FAIRIES AND
FANTASY IN WALES

SHORT STORIES FROM
THE MYTHICAL PAST
TO THE MODERN DAY

BY

VARIOUS AUTHORS

British Library Cataloguing-in-Publication Data
A catalogue record for this book is available from the
British Library

CONTENTS

OUT OF THE EARTH

ARTHUR MACHEN

There was some sort of confused complaint during last August of the ill behaviour of the children at certain Welsh watering places. Such reports and vague rumours are most difficult to trace to their heads and fountains; none has better reason to know that than myself. I need not go over the old ground here, but I am afraid that many people are wishing by this time that they had never heard my name; again, a considerable number of estimable persons are concerning themselves gloomily enough, from my point of view, with my everlasting welfare. They write me letters, some in kindly remonstrance, begging me not to deprive poor, sick-hearted souls of what little comfort they possess amidst their sorrows. Others send me tracts and pink leaflets with allusions to 'the daughter of a well-known canon'; others again are violently and anonymously abusive. And then in open print, in fair book form, Mr. Begbie has dealt with me righteously but harshly, as I cannot but think.

Yet, it was all so entirely innocent, nay casual, on my part.

A poor linnet of prose, I did but perform my indifferent piping in the *Evening News* because I wanted to do so, because I felt that the story of 'The Bowmen' ought to be told. An inventor of fantasies is a poor creature, heaven knows, when all the world is at war; but I thought that no harm would be done, at any rate, if I bore witness, after the fashion of the fantastic craft, to my belief in the heroic glory of the English host who went back from Mons fighting and triumphing.

And then, somehow or other, it was as if I had touched a button and set in action a terrific, complicated mechanism of rumours that pretended to be sworn truth, of gossip that posed as evidence, of wild tarradiddles that good men most firmly believed. The supposed testimony of that 'daughter of a well-known canon' took parish magazines by storm, and equally enjoyed the faith of dissenting divines. The 'daughter' denied all knowledge of the matter, but people still quoted her supposed sure word; and the issues were confused with tales, probably true, of painful hallucinations and deliriums of our retreating soldiers, men fatigued and shattered to the very verge of death. It all became worse than the Russian myths, and as in the fable of the Russians, it seemed impossible to follow the streams of delusion to their fountain-head – or heads, who was it who said that 'Miss M knew two officers who, etc., etc.'? I suppose we shall never know his lying, deluding name.

And so, I dare say, it will be with this strange affair of the troublesome children of the Welsh seaside town, or rather of a group of small towns and villages lying within a certain section or zone, which I am not going to indicate more precisely than I can help, since I love that country, and my recent experiences with 'The Bowmen' have taught me that no tale is too idle to be believed. And, of course, to begin with, nobody knew how this odd and malicious piece of gossip originated. So far as I know, it was more akin to the Russian myth than to the tale of 'The Angels of Mons'. That is, rumour preceded print; the thing was talked of here and there and passed from letter to letter long before the papers were aware of its existence. And – here it resembles rather the Mons affair – London and Manchester, Leeds and Birmingham were muttering vague unpleasant things while the little villages concerned basked innocently in the sunshine of an unusual prosperity.

In this last circumstance, as some believe, is to be sought the root of the whole matter. It is well known that certain east coast towns suffered from the dread of air-raids, and that a good many of their usual visitors went westward for the first time. So there is a theory that the east coast was mean enough to circulate reports against the west coast out of pure malice and envy. It may be so; I do not pretend to know. But here is a personal experience, such as it is, which illustrated the way in which the rumour was circulated. I was lunching one day at my Fleet Street tavern – this was early in July – and a friend of mine, a solicitor, of Serjeants' Inn, came in and sat at the same table. We began to talk of holidays and my friend Eddis asked me where I was going. 'To the same old place,' I said. 'Manavon. You know we always go there.' 'Are you really?' said the lawyer; 'I thought that coast had gone off a lot. My wife has a friend who's heard that it's not at all what it was.'

I was astonished to hear this, not seeing how a little village like Manavon could have 'gone off'. I had known it for ten years as having accommodation for about twenty visitors, and I could not believe that rows of lodging houses had sprung up since the August of 1914. Still I put the question to Eddis: 'Trippers?' I asked, knowing firstly that trippers hate the solitudes of the country and the sea; secondly, that there are no industrial towns within cheap and easy distance, and thirdly, that the railways were issuing no excursion tickets during the war.

'No, not exactly trippers,' the lawyer replied. 'But my wife's friend knows a clergyman who says that the beach at Tremaen is not at all pleasant now, and Tremaen's only a few miles from Manavon, isn't it?'

'In what way not pleasant?' I carried on my examination. 'Pierrots and shows, and that sort of thing?' I felt that it could not be so, for the solemn rocks of Tremaen would have turned the liveliest Pierrot to stone. He would have frozen into a crag on the beach, and the seagulls would carry away his song and make it a lament by lonely, booming caverns that look on Avalon. Eddis said he had heard nothing about showmen, but he understood that since the war the children of the whole district had gone quite out of hand.

'Bad language, you know,' he said, 'and all that sort of thing, worse than London slum children. One doesn't want one's wife and children to hear foul talk at any time, much less on their holiday. And they say that Castell Coch is quite impossible; no decent woman would be seen there!'

I said: 'Really, that's a great pity,' and changed the subject. But I could not make it out at all. I knew Castell Coch well – a little bay bastioned by dunes and red sandstone cliffs, rich with greenery. A stream of cold water runs down there to the sea; there is the ruined Norman Castle, the ancient church and the scattered village; it is altogether a place of peace and quiet and great beauty. The people there, children and grown-ups alike, were not merely decent but courteous folk: if one thanked a child for opening a gate, there would come the inevitable response: 'And welcome kindly, sir.' I could not make it out at all. I didn't believe the lawyer's tales; for the life of me I could not see what he could be driving at. And, for the avoidance of all unnecessary mystery, I may as well say that my wife and child and myself went down to Manavon last August and had a most delightful holiday. At the time we were certainly conscious of no annoyance or unpleasantness of any kind. Afterwards, I confess, I heard a story that puzzled and still puzzles me, and this story, if it be received, might give its own interpretation to one or two circumstances which seemed in themselves quite insignificant.

But all through July I came upon traces of evil rumours affecting this most gracious corner of the earth. Some of these rumours were repetitions of Eddis's gossip; others amplified his vague story and made it more definite. Of course, no first-hand evidence was available. There never is any first-hand evidence in these cases. But A knew B who had heard from C that her second cousin's little girl had been set upon and beaten by a pack of young Welsh savages. Then people quoted 'a doctor in large practice in a well-known town in the Midlands', to the effect that Tremaen was a sink of juvenile depravity. They said that a responsible medical man's evidence was final and convincing; but they didn't bother to find out who the doctor was, or whether there was any doctor at all – or any doctor relevant to the issue. Then the thing began to get into the papers in a sort of oblique, by-the-way sort of manner. People cited the case of these imaginary bad children in support of their educational views. One side said that 'these unfortunate little ones' would have been quite well behaved if they had no education at all; the opposition declared that continuation schools would speedily reform them and make them into admirable citizens. Then the poor Arfonshire children seemed to become involved in quarrels about Welsh disestablishment and in the question of the miners; and all the while they were going about behaving politely and admirably as they always do behave. I knew all the time that it was all nonsense, but I couldn't understand in the least what it meant, or who was pulling the wires of rumour, or their purpose in so pulling. I began to wonder whether the pressure and anxiety and suspense of a terrible war had unhinged the public mind, so that it was ready to believe any fable, to debate the reasons for happenings which had never happened. At last, quite incredible things began to be whispered: visitors' children had not only been beaten, they had been tortured; a little boy had been found impaled on a stake in a lonely field near Manavon; another child had been lured to destruction over the cliffs at Castell Coch. A London paper sent a good man down quietly to Arfon to investigate. He was away for a week, and at the end of that period returned to his office and in his own phrase, 'threw the whole story down'. There was not a word of truth, he said, in any of these rumours, no vestige of a foundation for the mildest forms of all this gossip. He had never seen such a beautiful country; he had never met pleasanter men, women or children; there was not a single case of anyone having been annoyed or troubled in any sort of fashion.

Yet all the while the story grew, and grew more monstrous and incredible. I was too much occupied in watching the progress of my own mythological monster to pay much attention. The town clerk of Tremaen, to which the legend had at length penetrated, wrote a brief letter to the press indignantly denying that there was the slightest foundation for 'the unsavoury rumours' which, he understood, were being circulated; and about this time we went down to Manavon and, as I say, enjoyed ourselves extremely. The weather was perfect: blues of paradise in the skies, the seas all a shimmering wonder, olive greens and emeralds, rich purples, glassy sapphires changing by the rocks; far away a haze of magic lights and colours at the meeting of sea and sky. Work and anxiety had harried me; I found nothing better than to rest on the thymy banks by the shore, finding an infinite balm and refreshment in the great sea before me, in the tiny flowers beside me. Or we would rest all the summer afternoon on a 'shelf' high on the grey cliffs and watch the tide creaming and surging about the rocks, and listen to it booming in the hollows and caverns below. Afterwards, as I say, there were one or two things that struck cold. But at the time those were nothing. You see a man in an odd white hat pass by and think little or nothing about it. Afterwards, when you hear that a man wearing just such a hat had committed murder in the next street five minutes before, then you find in that hat a certair interest and significance. 'Funny children,' was the phrase my little boy used; and I began to think they were 'funny' indeed.

If there be a key at all to this queer business, I think it is to be found in a talk I had not long ago with a friend of mine named Morgan. He is a Welshman and a dreamer, and some people say he is like a child who has grown up and yet has not grown up like other children of men. Though I did not know it, while I was at Manavon, he was spending his holiday time at Castell Coch. He was a lonely man and he liked lonely places, and when we met in the autumn he told me how, day after day, he would carry his bread and cheese and beer in a basket to a remote headland on that coast known as the Old Camp. Here, far above the waters, are solemn, mighty walls, turf-grown; circumvallations rounded and smooth with the passing of many thousand years. At one end of this most ancient place there is a tumulus, a tower of observation, perhaps, and underneath it slinks the green, deceiving ditch that seems to wind into the heart of the camp, but in reality rushes down to sheer rock and a precipice over the waters.

Here came Morgan daily, as he said, to dream of Avalon,

to purge himself from the fuming corruption of the streets.

And so, as he told me, it was with singular horror that one afternoon as he dozed and dreamed and opened his eyes now and again to watch the miracle and magic of the sea, as he listened to the myriad murmurs of the waves, his meditation was broken by a sudden burst of horrible raucous cries – and the cries of children, too, but children of the lowest type. Morgan says that the very tones made him shudder – 'They were to the ear what slime is to the touch,' and then the words: every foulness, every filthy abomination of speech; blasphemies that struck like blows at the sky, that sank down into the pure, shining depths, defiling them! He was amazed. He peered over the green wall of the fort, and there in the ditch he saw a swarm of noisome children, horrible little stunted creatures with old men's faces, with bloated faces, with little sunken eyes, with leering eyes. It was worse than uncovering a brood of snakes or a nest of worms.

No; he would not describe what they were about. 'Read about Belgium,' said Morgan, 'and think they couldn't have been more than five or six years old.' There was no infamy, he said, that they did not perpetrate; they spared no horror of cruelty. 'I saw blood running in streams, as they shrieked with laughter, but I could not find the mark of it on the grass afterwards.'

Morgan said he watched them and could not utter a word;

it was as if a hand held his mouth tight. But at last he found his voice and shrieked at them, and they burst into a yell of obscene laughter and shrieked back at him, and scattered out of sight. He could not trace them; he supposes that they hid in the deep bracken behind the Old Camp.

'Sometimes I can't understand my landlord at Castell Coch,' Morgan went on. 'He's the village postmaster and has a little farm of his own – a decent, pleasant, ordinary sort of chap. But now and again he will talk oddly. I was telling him about these beastly children and wondering who they could be when he broke into Welsh, something like "the battle that is for age unto ages; and the People take delight in it".'

So far Morgan, and it was evident that he did not understand at all. But this strange tale of his brought back an odd circumstance or two that I recollected: a matter of our little boy straying away more than once, and getting lost among the sand dunes and coming back screaming, evidently frightened horribly, and babbling about 'funny children'. We took no notice; did not trouble, I think, to look whether there were any children wandering about the dunes or not. We were accustomed to his small imaginations.

But after hearing Morgan's story I was interested and I wrote an account of the matter to my friend, old Doctor Duthoit, of Hereford. And he replied:

'They were only visible, only audible to children and the

child-like. Hence the explanation of what puzzled you at first; the rumours, how did they arise? They arose from nursery gossip, from scraps and odds and ends of half-articulate children's talk of horrors that they didn't understand, of words that shamed their nurses and their mothers.

'These little people of the earth rise up and rejoice in these times of ours. For they are glad, as the Welshman said, when they know that men follow their ways.'

THE LIVING DEAD MAN

Walter Map

I know of a strange portent that occurred in Wales, and concerns a dead man who walked by night and caused those he summoned to die of a dreadful sickness.

William Laudun or Landun, an English knight, strong of body and of proven valour, came to Gilbert Foliot, then Bishop of Hereford, now of London, and said,

'My Lord, I come to you for advice. A Welshman of evil life died of late unchristianly enough in my village, and straightway after four nights took to coming back every night to the village, and will not desist from summoning singly and by name his fellow villagers, who upon being called at once fall sick and die within three days, so that now there are very few of them left.'

The Bishop, marvelling, said: 'Peradventure the Lord has given power to the evil angel of that lost soul to move about in the dead corpse. However, let the body be exhumed, cut the neck through with a spade, and sprinkle the body and the grave well with holy water and replace it.'

When this was done, the survivors were none the less plagued by the former illusion.

So one night when the summoner had now left but few alive, he called William himself, citing him thrice. He, however, bold and quick as he was, and awake to the situation, darted out with his sword drawn, and chased the demon, who fled, up to the grave and there, as he fell into it, clave his head to the neck.

From that hour the ravage of that wandering pestilence ceased, and did no more hurt either to William himself or to any one else.

ARTHUR AND GORLAGON

George Lyman Kittredge

At the City of the Legions, King Arthur was keeping the renowned festival of Pentecost, to which he invited the great men and nobles of the whole of his kingdom, and when the solemn rites had been duly performed he bade them to a banquet, furnished with everything thereto pertaining. And as they were joyfully partaking of the feast of rich abundance, Arthur, in his excessive joy, threw his arms around the Queen, who was sitting beside him, and embracing her, kissed her very affectionately in the sight of all. But she was dumbfounded at his conduct, and blushing deeply, looked up at him and asked why he had kissed her thus at such an unusual place and hour.

Arthur. Because amidst all my riches I have nothing so pleasing and amidst all my delights nothing so sweet, as thou art.

The Queen. Well, if, as you say, you love me so much, you evidently think that you know my heart and my affection.

Arthur. I doubt not that your heart is well disposed towards me, and I certainly think that your affection is absolutely known to me.

The Queen. Well, if, as you say, you love me so much, you acknowledge that you have never yet fathomed either the nature or the heart of a woman.

Arthur. I call heaven to witness that if up to now they have lain hid from me, I will exert myself, and sparing no pains, I will never taste food until by good hap I fathom them.

So when the banquet was ended Arthur called to him Caius, his server, and said, 'Caius, do you and Walwain my nephew mount your horses and accompany me on the business to which I am hastening. But let the rest remain and entertain my guests in my stead until I return.' Caius and Walwain at once mounted their horses as they were bidden and hastened with Arthur to a certain king famed for his wisdom, named Gargol, who reigned over the neighbouring country; and on the third day they reached a certain valley, quite worn out, for since leaving home they had not tasted food nor slept, but had ever ridden on uninterruptedly night and day. Now immediately on the further side of that valley there was a lofty mountain, surrounded by a pleasant wood, in whose recesses was visible a very strong fortress built of polished stone. And Arthur, when he saw it at a distance, commanded Caius to hasten on before him with all speed, and bring back word to him to whom the town belonged. So

Caius, urging on his steed, hastened forward and entered the fortress, and on his return met Arthur just as he was entering the outer trench, and told him that the town belonged to King Gargol, to whom they were making their way.

Now it so happened that King Gargol had just sat down at table to dine; and Arthur, entering his presence on horseback, courteously saluted him and those who were feasting with him. And King Gargol said to him, 'Who art thou? and from whence? And wherefore hast thou entered into our presence with such haste?'

Arthur. 'I am Arthur,' he replied, 'the King of Britain: and I wish to learn from you what are the *heart, the nature, and the ways of women,* for I have very often heard that you are well skilled in matters of this kind.'

Gargol. Yours is a weighty question, Arthur, and there are very few who know how to answer it. But take my advice now, dismount and eat with me, and rest today, for I see that you are overwrought with your toilsome journey; and tomorrow I will tell you what I know of the matter.

Arthur denied that he was overwrought, pledging himself withal that he would never eat until he had learnt what he was in search of. At last, however, pressed by the King and by the company who were feasting with him, he assented, and, having dismounted, he sat at table on the seat which had been placed for him opposite the King. But as soon as it was dawn, Arthur, remembering the promise which had been made to him, went to King Gargol and said, 'O my dear King, make known to me, I beg, that which you promised yesterday you would tell me today.'

Gargol. You are displaying your folly, Arthur. Until now I thought you were a wise man: as to the heart, the nature, and the ways of woman, no one ever had a conception of what they are, and I do not know that I can give you any information on the subject. But I have a brother, King Torleil by name, whose kingdom borders on my own. He is older and wiser than I am: and indeed, if there is any one skilled in this matter, about which you are so anxious to know, I do not think it has escaped him. Seek him out, and desire him on my account to tell you what he knows of it.

So, having bidden Gargol farewell, Arthur departed, and instantly continuing his journey arrived after a four days' march at King Torleil's, and as it chanced found the King at dinner. And when the King had exchanged greetings with him and asked him who he was, Arthur replied that he was King of Britain, and had been sent to the King by his brother King Gargol, in order that the King might explain to him a matter, his ignorance of which had obliged him to approach the royal presence.

Torleil. What is it?

Arthur. I have applied my mind to investigate the heart,

the nature, and the ways of women, and have been unable to find anyone to tell me what they are. Do you therefore, to whom I have been sent, instruct me in these matters, and if they are known to you, do not keep them back from me.

Torleil. Yours is a weighty question, Arthur, and there are few who know how to answer it. Wherefore, as this is not the time to discuss such matters, dismount and eat, and rest today, and tomorrow I will tell you what I know about them.

Arthur replied, 'I shall be able to eat enough by-and-by. By my faith, I will never eat until I have learned that which I am in search of.' Pressed, however, by the King and by those who were sitting at table with him, he at length reluctantly consented to dismount, and sat down at the table opposite the King. But in the morning he came to King Torleil and began to ask him to tell what he had promised. Torleil confessed that he knew absolutely nothing about the matter, and directed Arthur to his third brother, King Gorlagon, who was older than himself, telling him that he had no doubt that Gorlagon was mighty in the knowledge of the things he was inquiring into, if indeed it was certain that anyone had any knowledge of them.

So Arthur hastened without delay to his destined goal, and after two days reached the city where King Gorlagon dwelt, and, as it chanced, found him at dinner, as he had found the others.

After greetings had been exchanged Arthur made known who he was and why he had come, and as he kept on asking for information on the matters about which he had come, King Gorlagon answered, 'Yours is a weighty question. Dismount and eat: and tomorrow I will tell you what you wish to know.'

But Arthur said he would by no means do that, and when again requested to dismount, he swore by an oath that he would yield to no entreaties until he had learned what he was in search of. So when King Gorlagon saw that he could not by any means prevail upon him to dismount, he said, 'Arthur, since you persist in your resolve to take no food until you know what you ask of me, although the labour of telling you the tale be great, and there is little use in telling it, yet I will relate to you what happened to a certain king, and thereby you will be able to test the heart, the nature, and the ways of women. Yet, Arthur, I beg you, dismount and eat, for yours is a weighty question and few there are who know how to answer it, and when I have told you my tale you will be but little the wiser.

Arthur. Tell on as you have proposed, and speak no more of my eating.

Gorlagon. Well, let your companions dismount and eat.

Arthur. Very well, let them do so.

So when they had seated themselves at table, King Gorlagon said, 'Arthur, since you are so eager to hear this business, give ear, and keep in mind what I am about to tell you.'

There was a king well known to me, noble, accomplished, rich, and far-famed for justice and for truth. He had provided for himself a delightful garden which had no equal, and in it he had caused to be sown and planted all kinds of trees and fruits, and spices of different sorts: and among the other shrubs which grew in the garden there was a beautiful slender sapling of exactly the same height as the King himself, which broke forth from the ground and began to grow on the same night and at the same hour as the King was born. Now concerning this sapling, it had been decreed by fate that whoever should cut it down, and striking his head with the slenderer part of it, should say, 'Be a wolf and have the understanding of a wolf,' he would at once become a wolf, and have the understanding of a wolf. And for this reason the King watched the sapling with great care and with great diligence, for he had no doubt that his safety depended upon it. So he surrounded the garden with a strong and steep wall, and allowed no one but the guardian, who was a trusted friend of his own, to be admitted into it; and it was his custom to visit that sapling three or four times a day, and to partake of no food until he had visited it, even

25

though he should fast until the evening. So it was that he alone understood this matter thoroughly.

Now this king had a very beautiful wife, but though fair to look upon, she did not prove chaste, and her beauty was the cause of her undoing. For she loved a youth, the son of a certain pagan king; and preferring his love to that of her lord, she had taken great pains to involve her husband in some danger so that the youth might be able lawfully to enjoy the embraces for which he longed. And observing that the King entered the garden so many times a day, and desiring to know the reason, she often purposed to question him on the subject, but never dared to do so. But at last one day, when the King had returned from hunting later than usual, and according to his wont had entered the plantation alone, the Queen, in her thirst for information, and unable to endure that the thing should be concealed from her any longer (as it is customary for a woman to wish to know everything), when her husband had returned and was seated at table, asked him with a treacherous smile why he went to the garden so many times a day, and had been there even then late in the evening before taking food. The King answered that that was a matter which did not concern her, and that he was under no obligation to divulge it to her; whereupon she became furious, and improperly suspecting that he was in the habit of consorting with an adulteress in the garden, cried out, 'I call all the gods of heaven to witness that I will never eat with you henceforth until you tell me the reason.' And rising suddenly from the table she went to her bedchamber, cunningly feigning sickness, and lay in bed for three days without taking any food.

On the third day, the King, perceiving her obstinacy and fearing that her life might be endangered in consequence, began to beg and exhort her with gentle words to rise and eat, telling her that the thing she wished to know was a secret which he would never dare to tell anyone. To which she replied, 'You ought to have no secrets from your wife, and you must know for certain that I would rather die than live, so long as I feel that I am so little loved by you,' and he could not by any means persuade her to take refreshment. Then the King, in too changeable and irresolute a mood and too devoted in his affection for his wife, explained to her how the matter stood, having first exacted an oath from her that she would never betray the secret to anyone, and would keep the sapling as sacred as her own life.

The Queen, however, having got from him that which she had so dearly wished and prayed for, began to promise him greater devotion and love, although she had already conceived in her mind a device by which she might bring about the crime she had been so long deliberating. So on the following day, when the King had gone to the woods to hunt, she seized an axe, and secretly entering the garden, cut down the sapling to the ground, and carried it away with her. When, however, she found that the King was returning, she concealed the sapling under her sleeve, which hung down long and loose, and went to the threshold of the door to meet him, and throwing her arms around him she embraced him as though she would have kissed him; and then suddenly thrust the sapling out from her sleeve and struck him on the head with it once and again, crying, 'Be a wolf, be a wolf', meaning to add 'and have the understanding of a wolf', but she added instead the words 'have the understanding of a man'. Nor was there any delay, but it came about as she had said; and he fled quickly to the woods with the hounds she set on him in pursuit, but his human understanding remained unimpaired.

Arthur, see, you have now learned in part the heart, the nature, and the ways of woman. Dismount now and eat, and afterwards I will relate at greater length what remains. For yours is a weighty question, and there are few who know how to answer it, and when I have told you all you will be but little the wiser.

Arthur. The matter goes very well and pleases me much. Follow up, follow up what you have begun.

Gorlagon. You are pleased then to hear what follows. Be attentive and I will proceed.

Then the Queen, having put to flight her lawful husband, at once summoned the young man of whom I have spoken, and having handed over to him the reins of government, became his wife. But the wolf, after roaming for a space of two years in the recesses of the woods to which he had fled, allied himself with a wild she-wolf, and begot two cubs by her. And remembering the wrong done him by his wife (as he was still possessed of his human understanding), he anxiously considered if he could in any way take his revenge upon her. Now near that wood there was a fortress at which the Queen was very often wont to sojourn with the King. And so this human wolf, looking out for his opportunity, took his she-wolf with her cubs one evening, and rushed unexpectedly into the town, and finding the two little boys of whom the aforesaid youth had become the father by his wife, playing by chance under the tower without anyone to guard them, he attacked and slew them, tearing them cruelly limb from limb. When the bystanders saw too late what had happened they pursued the wolves with shouts. The wolves, when what they had done was made known, fled swiftly away and escaped in safety. The Queen, however, overwhelmed with sorrow at the calamity, gave orders to her retainers to keep a careful watch for the return of the wolves. No long time had elapsed when the wolf, thinking that he was not yet satisfied, again visited the town with his companions, and meeting with two noble counts, brothers of the Queen, playing at the very gates of the palace, he attacked them, and tearing out their bowels gave them over to a frightful death. Hearing the noise, the servants assembled, and shutting the doors caught the cubs and hanged them. But the wolf, more cunning than the rest, slipped out of the hands of those who were holding him and escaped unhurt.

The wolf, overwhelmed with very great grief for the loss of his cubs and maddened by the greatness of his sorrow, made nightly forays against the flocks and herds of that province, and attacked them with such great slaughter that all the inhabitants, placing in ambush a large pack of hounds, met together to hunt and catch him; and the wolf, unable to endure these daily vexations, made for a neighbouring country and there began to carry on his usual ravages. However, he was at once chased from thence by the inhabitants, and compelled to go to a third country: and now he began to vent his rage with implacable fury, not only against the beasts but also against human beings. Now it chanced that a king was reigning over that country, young in years, of a mild disposition, and far-famed for his wisdom and industry: and when the countless destruction both of men and beasts wrought by the wolf was reported to him, he appointed a day on which he would set about to track and hunt the brute with a strong force of huntsmen and hounds.

For so greatly was the wolf held in dread that no one dared to go to rest anywhere around, but everyone kept watch the whole night long against his inroads.

So one night when the wolf had gone to a neighbouring village, greedy for bloodshed, and was standing under the eaves of a certain house listening intently to a conversation that was going on within, it happened that he heard the man nearest him tell how the King had proposed to seek and track him down on the following day, much being added as to the clemency and kindness of the King. When the wolf heard this he returned trembling to the recesses of the woods, deliberating what would be the best course for him to pursue.

In the morning the huntsmen and the King's retinue with an immense pack of hounds entered the woods, making the trees ring with the blast of horns and with shouting; and the King, accompanied by two of his intimate friends, followed at a more moderate pace. The wolf concealed himself near the road where the King was to pass, and when all had gone by and he saw the King approaching (for he judged from his countenance that it was the King) he dropped his head and ran close after him, and encircling the King's right foot with his paws he would have licked him affectionately like a suppliant asking for pardon, with such groanings as he was capable of. Then two noblemen who were guarding the King's person, seeing this enormous wolf (for they had never seen any of so vast a size), cried out, 'Master, see, here is the wolf we seek! see, here is the wolf we seek! strike him, slay him, do not let the hateful beast attack us!' The wolf, utterly fearless of their cries, followed close after the King, and kept licking him gently. The King was wonderfully moved, and after looking at the wolf for some time and perceiving that there was no fierceness in him, but that he was rather like one who craved for pardon, was much astonished, and commanded that none of his men should dare to inflict any harm on him, declaring that he had detected some signs of human understanding in him; so putting down his right hand to caress the wolf he gently stroked his head and scratched his ears. Then the King seized the wolf and endeavoured to lift him up to him. But the wolf, perceiving that the King was desirous of lifting him up, leapt up, and joyfully sat upon the neck of the charger in front of the King.

The King recalled his followers, and returned home. He had not gone far when lo! a stag of vast size met him in the forest pasture with antlers erect. Then the King said, 'I will try if there is any worth or strength in my wolf, and whether he can accustom himself to obey my commands.' And crying out he set the wolf upon the stag and thrust him from him with his hand. The wolf, well knowing how to capture this kind of prey, sprang up and pursued the stag, and getting in front of it attacked it, and catching it by the throat laid it dead in sight of the King. Then the King called him back and said, 'Of a truth you must be kept alive and not killed, seeing that you know how to show such service to us.' And taking the wolf with him he returned home.

So the wolf remained with the King, and was held in very great affection by him. Whatever the King commanded him he performed, and he never showed any fierceness towards or inflicted any hurt upon anyone. He daily stood at table before the King at dinner time with his forepaws erect, eating of his bread and drinking from the same cup. Wherever the King went he accompanied him, so that even at night he would not go to rest anywhere save beside his master's couch.

Now it happened that the King had to go on a long journey outside his kingdom to confer with another king, and to go at once, as it would be impossible for him to return in less than ten days. So he called his Queen, and said, 'As I must go on this journey at once, I commend this wolf to your protection, and I command you to keep him in my stead, if he will stay, and to minister to his wants.' But the Queen already hated the wolf because of the great sagacity which she had detected in him (and as it so often happens that the wife hates whom the husband loves), and she said, 'My lord, I am afraid that when you are gone he will attack me in the night if he lies in his accustomed place and will leave me mangled.' The King replied, 'Have no fear of that, for I have detected no such symptom in him all the long time he has been with me. However, if you have any doubt of it, I will have a chain made and will have him fastened up to my bed-ladder.' So the King gave orders that a chain of gold should be made, and when the wolf had been fastened up by it to the steps, he hastened away to the business he had on hand.

So the King set out, and the wolf remained with the Queen. But she did not show the care for him which she ought to have done. For he always lay chained up, though the King had commanded that he should be chained up at night only. Now the Queen loved the King's sewer with an unlawful love, and went to visit him whenever the King was absent. So on the eighth day after the King had started, they met in the bedchamber at midday and mounted the bed together, little heeding the presence of the wolf. And when the wolf saw them rushing into each other's impious embraces he blazed forth with fury, his eyes reddening, and the hair on his neck standing up, and he began to make as though he would attack them, but was held back by the chain by which he was fastened. And when he saw they had no intention of desisting from the iniquity on which they had embarked, he gnashed his teeth, and dug up the ground with his paws, and venting his rage over all his body, with awful howls he stretched the chain with such violence that it snapped in two. When loose he rushed with fury upon the sewer and threw him from the bed, and tore him so savagely that he left him half-dead. But to the Queen he did no harm at all, but only gazed upon her with venom in his eye. Hearing the mournful groans of the sewer, the servants tore the door from its hinges and rushed in. When asked the cause of all the tumult, that cunning Queen concocted a lying story, and told the servants that the wolf had devoured her son, and had torn the sewer as they saw while he was attempting to rescue the little one from death, and that he would have treated her in the same way had they not arrived in time to succour her. So the sewer was brought half dead to the guest-chamber. But the Queen fearing that the King might somehow discover the truth of the matter, and considering how she might take her revenge on the wolf, shut up the child, whom she had represented as having been devoured by the wolf, along with his nurse in an underground room far removed from any access; every one being under the impression that he had in fact been devoured.

After these events news was brought to the Queen that the King was returning sooner than had been expected. So the deceitful woman, full of cunning, went forth to meet him with her hair cut close, and cheeks torn, and garments splashed with blood, and when she met him cried, 'Alas! Alas! Alas! my lord, wretched that I am, what a loss have

I sustained during your absence!' At this the King was dumbfounded, and asked what was the matter, and she replied, 'That wretched beast of yours, of yours I say, which I have but too truly suspected all this time, has devoured your son in my lap; and when your sewer was struggling to come to the rescue the beast mangled and almost killed him, and would have treated me in the same way had not the servants broken in; see here the blood of the little one splashed upon my garments is witness of the thing.' Hardly had she finished speaking, when lo! the wolf hearing the King approach, sprang forth from the bedchamber, and rushed into the King's embraces as though he well deserved them, jumping about joyfully, and gambolling with greater delight than he had ever done before. At this the King, distracted by contending emotions, was in doubt what he should do, on the one hand reflecting that his wife would not tell him an untruth, on the other that if the wolf had been guilty of so great a crime against him he would undoubtedly not have dared to meet him with such joyful bounds.

So while his mind was driven hither and thither on these matters and he refused food, the wolf sitting close by him touched his foot gently with his paw, and took the border of his cloak into his mouth, and by a movement of the head invited him to follow him. The King, who understood the wolf's customary signals, got up and followed him through the different bedchambers to the underground room where the boy was hidden away. And finding the door bolted the wolf knocked three or four times with his paw, as much as to ask that it might be opened to him. But as there was some delay in searching for the key—for the Queen had hidden it away—the wolf, unable to endure the delay, drew back a little, and spreading out the claws of his four paws he rushed headlong at the door, and driving it in, threw it down upon the middle of the floor broken and shattered. Then running forward he took the infant from its cradle in his shaggy arms, and gently held it up to the King's face for a kiss.

The King marvelled and said, 'There is something beyond this which is not clear to my comprehension.' Then he went out after the wolf, who led the way, and was conducted by him to the dying sewer; and when the wolf saw the sewer, the King could scarcely restrain him from rushing upon him. Then the King sitting down in front of the sewer's couch, questioned him as to the cause of his sickness, and as to the accident which had occasioned his wounds. The only confession, however, he would make was that in rescuing the boy from the wolf, the wolf had attacked him; and he called the Queen to witness to the truth of what he said. The King in answer said, 'You are evidently lying: my son lives: he was not dead at all, and now that I have found him and have convicted both you and the Queen of treachery to me, and of forging lying tales, I am afraid that something else may be false also. I know the reason why the wolf, unable to bear his master's disgrace, attacked you so savagely, contrary to his wont. Therefore confess to me at once the truth of the matter, else I swear by the Majesty of highest Heaven that I will deliver thee to the flames to burn.' Then the wolf making an attack upon him pressed him close, and would have mangled him again had he not been held back by the bystanders.

What need of many words? When the King insisted, sometimes with threats, sometimes with coaxing, the sewer confessed the crime of which he had been guilty, and humbly prayed to be forgiven. But the King, blazing out in an excess of fury, delivered the sewer up to be kept in prison, and immediately summoned the chief men from the whole of his kingdom to meet, and through them he held an investigation into the circumstances of this great crime. Sentence was given. The sewer was flayed alive and hanged. The Queen was torn limb from limb by horses and thrown into balls of flame.

After these events the King pondered over the extraordinary sagacity and industry of the wolf with close attention and great persistence, and afterwards discussed the subject more fully with his wise men, asserting that a being who was clearly endued with such great intelligence must have the understanding of a man, 'for no beast,' he argued, 'was ever found to possess such great wisdom, or to show such great devotion to any one as this wolf has shown to me. For he understands perfectly whatever we say to him: he does what he is ordered: he always stands by me, wherever I may be: he rejoices when I rejoice, and when I am in sorrow, he sorrows too. And you must know that one who has avenged with such severity the wrong which has been done me must undoubtedly have been a man of great sagacity and ability, and must have assumed the form of a wolf under some spell or incantation.'

At these words the wolf, who was standing by the King, showed great joy, and licking his hands and feet and pressing close to his knees, showed by the expression of his countenance and the gesture of his whole body that the King had spoken the truth.

Then the King said, 'See with what gladness he agrees with what I say, and shows by unmistakable signs that I have spoken the truth. There can now be no further doubt about the matter, and would that power might be granted me to discover whether by some act or device I might be able to restore him to his former state, even at the cost of my worldly substance; nay, even at the risk of my life.' So, after long deliberation, the King at length determined that the wolf should be sent off to go before him, and to take whatever direction he pleased whether by land or by sea. 'For perhaps,' said he, 'if we could reach his country we might get to know what has happened and find some remedy for him.'

So the wolf was allowed to go where he would, and they all followed after him. And he at once made for the sea, and impetuously dashed into the waves as though he wished to cross. Now his own country adjoined that region, being, however, separated from it on one side by the sea, though in another direction it was accessible by land, but by a longer route. The King, seeing that he wished to cross over, at once gave orders that the fleet should be launched and that the army should assemble.

So the King, having ordered his ship, and duly equipped his army, approached the sea with a great force of soldiers, and on the third day he landed safely at the wolf's country; and when they reached the shore the wolf was the first to leap from the ship, and clearly signified to them by his customary nod and gesture that this was his country. Then the King, taking some of his men with him, hastened secretly to a certain neighbouring city, commanding his army to remain on ship until he had looked into the affair and returned to them. However, he had scarcely entered the city when the whole course of events became clear to him. For all the men of that province, both of high and low degree, were groaning under the intolerable tyranny of the king who had succeeded to the wolf, and were with one voice lamenting their master, who by the craft and subtlety of his wife had been changed into a wolf, remembering what a kind and gentle master he was.

So having discovered what he wanted to know, and having ascertained where the king of that province was then living, the King returned with all speed to his ships, marched out his troops, and attacking his adversary suddenly and unexpectedly, slew or put to flight all his defenders, and captured both him and his Queen and made them subject to his dominion.

So the King, relying on his victory, assembled a council of the chief men of the kingdom, and setting the Queen in the sight of them all, said, 'O most perfidious and wicked of women, what madness induced you to plot such great treachery against your lord! But I will not any longer bandy words with one who has been judged unworthy of intercourse with anyone; so answer the question I put to you at once, for I will certainly cause you to die of hunger and thirst and exquisite tortures, unless you show me where the sapling lies hidden with which you transformed your husband into a wolf. Perhaps the human shape which he has lost may thereby be recovered.' Whereupon she swore that she did not know where the sapling was, saying that it was well known that it had been broken up and burnt in the fire.

However, as she would not confess, the King handed her over to the tormentors, to be daily tortured and daily exhausted with punishments, and allowed neither food nor drink. So at last, compelled by the severity of her punishment, she produced the sapling and handed it to the King.

And the King took it from her, and with glad heart brought the wolf forward into the midst, and striking his head with the thicker part of the sapling, added these words, 'Be a man and have the understanding of a man.' And no sooner were the words spoken than the effect followed. The wolf became a man as he had been before, though far more beautiful and comely, being now possessed of such grace that one could at once detect that he was a man of great nobility. The King seeing a man of such great beauty metamorphosed from a wolf standing before him, and pitying the wrongs the man had suffered, ran forward with great joy and embraced him, kissing and lamenting him and shedding tears. And as they embraced each other they drew such long protracted sighs and shed so many tears that all the multitude standing around were constrained to weep. The one returned thanks for all the many kindnesses which had been shown him: the other lamented that he had behaved with less consideration than he ought. What more? Extraordinary joy is shown by all, and the King, having received the submission of the principal men, according to ancient custom, retook possession of his sovereignty. Then the adulterer and adulteress were brought into his presence, and he was consulted as to what he judged ought to be done with them. And he condemned the pagan king to death. The Queen he only divorced, but of his inborn clemency spared her life, though she well deserved to lose it. The other King, having been honoured and enriched with costly presents, as was befitting, returned to his own kingdom.

Now, Arthur, you have learned what the heart, the nature, and the ways of women are. Have a care for yourself and see if you are any the wiser for it. Dismount now and eat, for we have both well deserved our meal I, for the tale I have told, and you for listening to it.

Arthur. I will by no means dismount until you have answered the question I am about to ask you.

Gorlagon. What is that?

Arthur. Who is that woman sitting opposite you of a sad countenance, and holding before her in a dish a human head bespattered with blood, who has wept whenever you have smiled, and who has kissed the bloodstained head whenever you have kissed your wife during the telling of your tale?

Gorlagon. If this thing were known to me alone, Arthur (he replied), I would by no means tell it you; but as it is well known to all who are sitting at table with me, I am not ashamed that you also should be made acquainted with it.

43

That woman who is sitting opposite me, she it was who, as I have just told you, wrought so great a crime against her lord, that is to say against myself. In me you may recognise that wolf who, as you have heard, was transformed first from a man into a wolf, and then from a wolf into a man again. When I became a wolf it is evident that the kingdom to which I first went was that of my middle brother, King Torleil. And the King who took such great pains to care for me you can have no doubt was my youngest brother, King Gargol, to whom you came in the first instance. And the bloodstained head which that woman sitting opposite me embraces in the dish she has in front of her is the head of that youth for love of whom she wrought so great a crime against me. For when I returned to my proper shape again, in sparing her life, I subjected her to this penalty only, namely, that she should always have the head of her paramour before her, and that when I kissed the wife I had married in her stead she should imprint kisses on him for whose sake she had committed that crime. And I had the head embalmed to keep it free from putrefaction. For I knew that no punishment could be more grievous to her than a perpetual exhibition of her great wickedness in the sight of all the world.

Arthur, dismount now, if you so desire, for now that I have invited you, you will, so far as I am concerned, from henceforth remain where you are.

So Arthur dismounted and ate, and on the following day returned home a nine days' journey, marvelling greatly at what he had heard.

THE FAIRY PEOPLE

Giraldus Cambrensis

A short time before our days, a circumstance worthy of
note occurred in these parts, which Elidorus, a priest, most
strenuously affirmed had befallen himself. When a youth of
twelve years, and learning his letters, since, as Solomon says,
'The root of learning is bitter, although the fruit is sweet,' in
order to avoid the discipline and frequent stripes inflicted
on him by his preceptor, he ran away, and concealed himself
under the hollow bank of a river.

After fasting in that situation for two days, two little men
of pigmy stature appeared to him, saying, 'If you will come
with us, we will lead you into a country full of delights and
sports.' Assenting and rising up, he followed his guides
through a path, at first subterraneous and dark, into a most
beautiful country, adorned with rivers and meadows, woods
and plains, but obscure, and not illuminated with the full
light of the sun. All the days were cloudy, and the nights
extremely dark, on account of the absence of the moon and
stars.

The boy was brought before the king, and introduced to him in the presence of the court; who, having examined him for a long time, delivered him to his son, who was then a boy. These men were of the smallest stature, but very well proportioned in their make; they were all of a fair complexion, with luxuriant hair falling over their shoulders like that of a woman. They had horses and greyhounds adapted to their size. They neither ate flesh nor fish, but lived on milk diet, made up into messes with saffron. They never took an oath, for they detested nothing so much as lies. As often as they returned from our upper hemisphere, they reprobated our ambition, infidelities, and inconstancies; they had no form of public worship, being strict lovers and reverers, as it seemed, of truth.

The boy frequently returned to our hemisphere, sometimes by the way he had first gone, sometimes by another: at first in company with other persons, and afterwards alone, and made himself known only to his mother, declaring to her the manners, nature, and state of that people. Being desired by her to bring a present of gold, with which that region abounded, he stole, while at play with the king's son, the golden ball with which he used to divert himself, and brought it to his mother in great haste; and when he reached the door of his father's house, but not unpursued, and was entering it in a great hurry, his foot stumbled on the threshold, and falling down into the room where his mother was sitting, the two pigmies seized the ball which had dropped from his hand, and departed, shewing the boy every mark of contempt and derision.

On recovering from his fall, confounded with shame, and execrating the evil counsel of his mother, he returned by the usual track to the subterraneous road, but found no appearance of any passage, though he searched for it on the banks of the river for nearly the space of a year. But since those calamities are often alleviated by time, which reason cannot mitigate, and length of time alone blunts the edge of our afflictions, and puts an end to many evils, the youth having been brought back by his friends and mother, and restored to his right way of thinking, and to his learning, in process of time attained the rank of priesthood.

Whenever David II, bishop of St David's, talked to him in his advanced state of life concerning this event, he could never relate the particulars without shedding tears. He had made himself acquainted with the language of that nation, the words of which, in his younger days, he used to recite, which, as the bishop often had informed me, were very conformable to the Greek idiom.

If a scrupulous inquirer should ask my opinion of the relation here inserted, I answer with Augustine, 'that the divine miracles are to be admired, not discussed'. Nor do I, by denial, place bounds to the divine power, nor, by assent, insolently extend what cannot be extended. But I always call to mind the saying of St Jerome; 'You will find,' says he, 'many things incredible and improbable, which nevertheless are true; for nature cannot in any respect prevail against the lord of nature.' These things, therefore, and similar contingencies, I should place, according to the opinion of Augustine, among those particulars which are neither to be affirmed, nor too positively denied.

THE CHRONIC ARGONAUTS

H. G. Wells

THE STORY FROM AN ESOTERIC POINT OF VIEW

Being the Account of Dr Nebogipfel's Sojourn in Llyddwdd

About half-a-mile outside the village of Llyddwdd by the road that goes up over the eastern flank of the mountain called Pen-y-pwll to Rwstog is a large farm-building known as the Manse. It derives this title from the fact that it was at one time the residence of the minister of the Calvinistic Methodists. It is a quaint, low, irregular erection, lying back some hundred yards from the railway, and now fast passing into a ruinous state.

Since its construction in the latter half of the last century this house has undergone many changes of fortune, having been abandoned long since by the farmer of the surrounding acres for less pretentious and more commodious headquarters. Among others Miss Carnot, 'the Gallic Sappho' at one time made it her home, and later on an old man named Williams became its occupier. The foul murder of this tenant by his two sons was the cause of its remaining for some considerable period uninhabited; with the inevitable consequence of its undergoing very extensive dilapidation.

The house had got a bad name, and adolescent man and Nature combined to bring swift desolation upon it. The fear of the Williamses which kept the Llyddwdd lads from gratifying their propensity to invade its deserted interior, manifested itself in unusually destructive resentment against its external breakables. The missiles with which they at once confessed and defied their spiritual dread, left scarcely a splinter of glass, and only battered relics of the old-fashioned leaden frames, in its narrow windows, while numberless shattered tiles about the house, and four or five black apertures yawning behind the naked rafters in the roof, also witnessed vividly to the energy of their trajection. Rain and wind thus had free way to enter the empty rooms and work their will there, old Time aiding and abetting. Alternately soaked and desiccated, the planks of flooring and wainscot warped apart strangely, split here and there, and tore themselves away in paroxysms of rheumatic pain from the rust-devoured nails that had once held them firm. The plaster of walls and ceiling, growing green-black with a rain-fed crust of lowly life, parted slowly from the fermenting laths; and large fragments thereof falling down inexplicably in tranquil hours, with loud concussion and clatter, gave strength to the popular superstition that old Williams and his sons were fated to re-enact their fearful tragedy until the final judgment. White roses and daedal creepers, that Miss Carnot had first adorned the walls with, spread now luxuriantly over the lichen-filmed tiles of the roof, and in slender graceful sprays timidly invaded the ghostly cobweb-draped apartments. Fungi, sickly pale, began to displace and uplift the bricks in the cellar floor; while on the rotting wood everywhere they clustered, in all the glory of the purple and mottled crimson, yellow-brown and hepatite. Woodlice and ants, beetles and moths, winged and creeping things innumerable, found each day a more congenial home among the ruins; and after them in ever-increasing multitudes swarmed the blotchy toads. Swallows and martins built every year more thickly in the silent, airy, upper chambers. Bats and owls struggled for the crepuscular corners of the lower rooms. Thus, in the Spring of the year eighteen hundred and eighty-seven, was Nature taking over, gradually but certainly, the tenancy of the old Manse. 'The house was falling into decay,' as men who do not appreciate the application of human derelicts to other beings' use would say, 'surely and swiftly.' But it was destined nevertheless to shelter another human tenant before its final dissolution.

There was no intelligence of the advent of a new inhabitant in quiet Llyddwdd. He came without a solitary premonition out of the vast unknown into the sphere of minute village observation and gossip. He fell into the Llyddwdd world, as it were, like a thunderbolt falling in the daytime. Suddenly, out of nothingness, he *was*. Rumour, indeed, vaguely averred that he was seen to arrive by a certain train from London, and to walk straight without hesitation to the old Manse, giving neither explanatory word nor sign to mortal as to his purpose there: but then the same fertile source of information also hinted that he was first beheld skimming down the slopes of steep Pen-y-pwll with exceeding swiftness, riding, as it appeared to the intelligent observer, upon an instrument not unlike a sieve and that he entered the house by the chimney. Of these conflicting reports, the former was the first to be generally circulated, but the latter, in view of the bizarre presence and eccentric ways of the newest inhabitant, obtained wider credence. By whatever means he arrived, there can be no doubt that he was in, and in possession of the Manse, on the first of May; because on the morning of that day he was inspected by Mrs Morgan ap Lloyd Jones, and subsequently by the numerous persons her report brought up the mountain slope, engaged in the curious occupation of nailing sheet-tin across the void window sockets of his new domicile—'blinding his house', as Mrs Morgan ap Lloyd Jones not inaptly termed it.

He was a small-bodied, sallow faced little man, clad in a close-fitting garment of some stiff, dark material, which Mr Parry Davies the Llyddwdd shoemaker, opined was leather. His aquiline nose, thin lips, high cheek-ridges, and pointed chin, were all small and mutually well proportioned; but the bones and muscles of his face were rendered excessively prominent and distinct by his extreme leanness. The same cause contributed to the sunken appearance of the large eager-looking grey eyes, that gazed forth from under his phenomenally wide and high forehead. It was this latter feature that most powerfully attracted the attention of an observer. It seemed to be great beyond all preconceived ratio to the rest of his countenance. Dimensions, corrugations, wrinkles, venation, were alike abnormally exaggerated. Below it his eyes glowed like lights in some cave at a cliff's foot. It so over-powered and suppressed the rest of his face as to give an *unhuman* appearance almost, to what would otherwise have been an unquestionably handsome profile. The lank black hair that hung unkempt before his eyes served to increase rather than conceal this effect, by adding to unnatural altitude a suggestion of hydrocephalic projection: and the idea of something ultra human was furthermore accentuated by the temporal arteries that pulsated visibly through his transparent yellow skin. No wonder, in view even of these things, that among the highly and over-poetical Cymric of Llyddwdd the sieve theory of arrival found considerable favour.

It was his bearing and actions, however, much more than his personality, that won over believers to the warlock notion of matters. In almost every circumstance of life the observant villagers soon found his ways were not only not *their* ways, but altogether inexplicable upon any theory of motives they could conceive. Thus, in a small matter at the beginning, when Arthur Price Williams, eminent and famous in every tavern in Caernarvonshire for his social gifts, endeavoured, in choicest Welsh and even choicer English, to inveigle the stranger into conversation over the sheet-tin performance, he failed utterly. Inquisitional supposition, straightforward enquiry, offer of assistance, suggestion of method, sarcasm, irony, abuse, and at last, gage of battle, though shouted with much effort from the road hedge, went unanswered and apparently unheard. Missile weapons, Arthur Price Williams found, were equally unavailing for the purpose of introduction, and the gathered crowd dispersed with unappeased curiosity and suspicion. Later in the day, the swarth apparition was seen striding down the mountain road towards the village, hatless, and with such swift width of step and set resolution of countenance, that Arthur Price Williams, beholding him from afar from the Pig and Whistle doorway was seized with dire consternation, and hid behind the Dutch oven in the kitchen till he was past. Wild panic also smote the school-house as the children were coming out, and drove them indoors like leaves before a gale. He was merely seeking the provision shop, however, and erupted thencefrom after a prolonged stay, loaded with a various armful of blue parcels, a loaf, herrings, pigs' trotters, salt pork, and a black bottle, with which he returned in the same swift projectile gait to the Manse. His way of shopping was to name, and to name simply, without solitary other word of explanation, civility or request, the article he required.

The shopkeeper's crude meteorological superstitions and inquisitive commonplaces, he seemed not to hear, and he might have been esteemed deaf if he had not evinced the promptest attention to the faintest relevant remark. Consequently it was speedily rumoured that he was determined to avoid all but the most necessary human intercourse. He lived altogether mysteriously, in the decaying manse, without mortal service or companionship, presumably sleeping on planks or litter, and either preparing his own food or eating it raw. This, coupled with the popular conception of the haunting patricides, did much to strengthen the popular supposition of some vast gulf between the newcomer and common humanity. The only thing that was inharmonious with this idea of severance from mankind was a constant flux of crates filled with grotesquely contorted glassware, cases of brazen and steel instruments, huge coils of wire, vast iron and fire-clay implements, of inconceivable purpose, jars and phials labelled in black and scarlet—POISON, huge packages of books, and gargantuan rolls of cartridge paper, which set in towards his Llyddwdd quarters from the outer world. The apparently hieroglyphic inscriptions on these various consignments revealed at the profound scrutiny of Pugh Jones that the style and title of the new inhabitant was Dr Moses Nebogipfel, Ph.D., F.R.S., N.W.R., PAID: at which discovery much edification was felt, especially among the purely Welsh-speaking community. Further than this, these arrivals, by their evident unfitness for any allowable mortal use, and inferential diabolicalness, filled the neighbourhood with a vague horror and lively curiosity, which were greatly augmented by the extraordinary phenomena, and still more extraordinary accounts thereof, that followed their reception in the Manse.

The first of these was on Wednesday, the fifteenth of May, when the Calvinistic Methodists of Llyddwdd had their annual commemoration festival; on which occasion, in accordance with custom, dwellers in the surrounding parishes of Rwstog, Pen-y-garn, Caergyllwdd, Llanrdd, and even distant Llanrwst flocked into the village. Popular thanks to Providence were materialised in the usual way, by means of plum-bread and butter, mixed tea, *terza*, consecrated flirtations, kiss-in-the-ring, rough-and-tumble football, and vituperative political speechmaking. About half-past eight the fun began to tarnish, and the assembly to break up; and by nine numerous couples and occasional groups were wending their way in the darkling along the hilly Llyddwdd and Rwstog road. It was a calm warm night; one of those nights when lamps, gas and heavy sleep seem stupid ingratitude to the Creator. The zenith sky was an ineffable deep lucent blue, and the evening star hung golden in the liquid darkness of the west. In the north-north-west, a faint phosphorescence marked the sunken day. The moon was just rising, pallid and gibbous over the huge haze-dimmed shoulder of Pen-y-pwll. Against the wan eastern sky, from the vague outline of the mountain slope, the Manse stood out black, clear and solitary. The stillness of the twilight had hushed the myriad murmurs of the day. Only the sounds of footsteps and voices and laughter, that came fitfully rising and falling from the roadway, and an intermittent hammering in the darkened dwelling, broke the silence. Suddenly a strange whizzing, buzzing whirr filled the night air, and a bright flicker glanced across the dim path of the wayfarers. All eyes were turned in astonishment to the old Manse. The house no longer loomed a black featureless block but was filled to overflowing with light. From the gaping holes in the roof, from chinks and fissures amid tiles and brickwork, from every gap which Nature or man had pierced in the crumbling old shell, a blinding blue-white glare was streaming, beside which the rising moon seemed a disc of opaque sulphur. The thin mist of the dewy night had caught the violet glow and hung, unearthly smoke, over the colourless blaze. A strange turmoil and outcrying in the old Manse now began, and grew ever more audible to the clustering spectators, and therewith came clanging loud impacts against the window-guarding tin. Then from the gleaming roof-gaps of the house suddenly vomited forth a wonderous swarm of heteromerous living things—swallows, sparrows, martins, owls, bats, insects in visible multitudes, to hang for many minutes a noisy, gyring, spreading cloud over the black gables and chimneys . . . and then slowly to thin out and vanish away in the night.

As this tumult died away the throbbing humming that had first arrested attention grew once more in the listener's hearing, until at last it was the only sound in the long stillness. Presently, however, the road gradually awoke again to the beating and shuffling of feet, as the knots of Rwstog people, one by one, turned their blinking eyes from the dazzling whiteness and, pondering deeply, continued their homeward way.

The cultivated reader will have already discerned that

this phenomenon, which sowed a whole crop of uncanny thoughts in the minds of these worthy folk, was simply the installation of the electric light in the Manse. Truly, this last vicissitude of the old house was its strangest one. Its revival to mortal life was like the raising of Lazarus. From that hour forth, by night and day, behind the tin-blinded windows, the tamed lightning illuminated every corner of its quickly changing interior. The almost frenzied energy of the lank-haired, leather-clad little doctor swept away into obscure holes and corners and common destruction, creeper sprays, toadstools, rose leaves, birds' nests, birds' eggs, cobwebs, and all the coatings and lovingly fanciful trimmings with which that maternal old dotard, Dame Nature, had tricked out the decaying house for its lying in state. The magneto-electric apparatus whirred incessantly amid the vestiges of the wainscoted dining-room, where once the eighteenth-century tenant had piously read morning prayer and eaten his Sunday dinner; and in the place of his sacred symbolical sideboard was a nasty heap of coke. The oven of the bakehouse supplied substratum and material for a forge, whose snorting, panting bellows, and intermittent, ruddy spark-laden blast made the benighted, but Bible-lit Welsh women murmur in liquid Cymric, as they hurried by: 'Whose breath kindleth coals, and out of his mouth is a flame of fire.' For the idea these good people formed of it was that a tame, but occasionally restive, leviathan had been added to the terrors of the haunted house. The constantly increasing accumulation of pieces of machinery, big brass castings, block tin, casks, crates, and packages of innumerable articles, by their demands for space, necessitated the sacrifice of most of the slighter partitions of the house, and the beams and flooring of the upper chambers were also mercilessly sawn away by the tireless scientist in such a way as to convert them into mere shelves and corner brackets of the atrial space between cellars and rafters. Some of the sounder planking was utilised in the making of a rude broad table, upon which files and heaps of geometrical diagrams speedily accumulated. The production of these latter seemed to be the object upon which the mind of Dr Nebogipfel was so inflexibly set. All other circumstances of his life were made entirely subsidiary to this one occupation. Strangely complicated traceries of lines they were—plans, elevations, sections by surfaces and solids, that, with the help of logarithmic mechanical apparatus and involved curvigraphical machines, spread swiftly under his expert hands over yard after yard of paper. Some of these symbolised shapes he despatched to London, and they presently returned, *realised*, in forms of brass and ivory, and nickel and mahogany. Some of them he himself translated into solid models of metal and wood; occasionally casting the metallic ones in moulds of sand, but often laboriously hewing them out of the block for greater precision of dimension. In this second process, among other appliances, he employed a steel circular saw set with diamond powder and made to rotate with extraordinary swiftness, by means of steam and multiplying gear. It was this latter thing, more than all else, that filled Llyddwdd with a sickly loathing of the Doctor as a man of blood and darkness. Often in the silence of midnight—for the newest inhabitant heeded the sun but little in his incessant research—the awakened dwellers around Pen-y-pwll would hear, what was at first a complaining murmur, like the groaning of a wounded man, '*gurr*-urr-urr-URR', rising by slow gradations in pitch and intensity to the likeness of a voice in despairing passionate protest, and at last ending abruptly in a sharp piercing shriek that rang in the ears for hours afterwards and begot numberless gruesome dreams.

The mystery of all these unearthly noises and inexplicable phenomena, the Doctor's inhumanly brusque bearing and evident uneasiness when away from his absorbing occupation, his entire and jealous seclusion, and his terrifying behaviour to certain officious intruders, roused popular resentment and curiously to the highest, and a plot was already on foot to make some sort of popular inquisition (probably accompanied by an experimental ducking) into his proceedings, when the sudden death of the hunchback

Hughes in a fit, brought matters to an unexpected crisis. It happened in broad daylight, in the roadway just opposite the Manse. Half a dozen people witnessed it. The unfortunate creature was seen to fall suddenly and roll about on the pathway, struggling violently, as it appeared to the spectators, with some invisible assailant. When assistance reached him he was purple in the face and his blue lips were covered with a glairy foam. He died almost as soon as they laid hands on him.

Owen Thomas, the general practitioner, vainly assured the excited crowd which speedily gathered outside the Pig and Whistle, whither the body had been carried, that death was unquestionably natural. A horrible zymotic suspicion had gone forth that the deceased was the victim of Dr Nebogipfel's imputed aerial powers. The contagion was with the news that passed like a flash through the village and set all Llyddwdd seething with a fierce desire for action against the worker of this iniquity. Downright superstition, which had previously walked somewhat modestly about the village, in the fear of ridicule and the Doctor, now appeared boldly before the sight of all men, clad in the terrible majesty of truth. People who had hitherto kept entire silence as to their fears of the imp-like philosopher suddenly discovered a fearsome pleasure in whispering dread possibilities to kindred souls, and from whispers of possibilities their sympathy-fostered utterances soon developed into unhesitating asserverations in loud and even high-pitched tones. The fancy of a captive leviathan, already alluded to, which had up to now been the horrid but secret joy of a certain conclave of ignorant old women, was published to all the world as indisputable fact; it being stated, on her own authority, that the animal had, on one occasion, chased Mrs Morgan ap Lloyd Jones almost into Rwstog. The story that Nebogipfel had been heard within the Manse chanting, in conjunction with the Williamses, horrible blasphemy, and that a 'black flapping thing, of the size of a young calf', had thereupon entered the gap in the roof, was universally believed in. A grisly anecdote, that owed its origination to a stumble in the churchyard, was circulated, to the effect that the Doctor had been caught ghoulishly tearing with his long white fingers at a new-made grave. The numerously attested declaration that Nebogipfel and the murdered Williams had been seen hanging the sons on a ghostly gibbet, at the back of the house, was due to the electric illumination of a fitfully wind-shaken tree. A hundred like stories hurtled thickly about the village and darkened the moral atmosphere. The Reverend Elijah Ulysses Cook, hearing of the tumult, sallied forth to allay it, and narrowly escaped drawing on himself the gathering lightning.

By eight o'clock (it was Monday the twenty-second of July) a grand demonstration had organised itself against the 'necromancer'. A number of bolder hearts among the men formed the nucleus of the gathering, and at nightfall Arthur Price Williams, John Peters, and others brought torches and raised their spark-raining flames aloft with curt ominous suggestions. The less adventurous village manhood came straggling late to the rendezvous, and with them the married women came in groups of four or five, greatly increasing the excitement of the assembly with their shrill hysterical talk and active imaginations. After these the children and young girls, overcome by undefinable dread, crept quietly out of the too silent and shadowy houses into the yellow glare of the pine knots, and the tumultuary noise of the thickening people. By nine, nearly half the Llyddwdd population was massed before the Pig and Whistle. There was a confused murmur of many tongues, but above all the stir and chatter of the growing crowd could be heard the coarse, cracked voice of the blood-thirsty old fanatic, Pritchard, drawing a congenial lesson from the fate of the four hundred and fifty idolators of Carmel.

Just as the church clock was beating out the hour, an occultly originated movement up hill began, and soon the whole assembly, men, women, and children, was moving in a fear-compacted mass, towards the ill-fated doctor's abode. As they left the brightly-lit public house behind them, a quavering female voice began singing one of those grim-sounding canticles that so satisfy the Calvinistic ear. In a wonderfully short time, the tune had been caught up, first by two or three, and then by the whole procession, and the manifold shuffling of heavy shoon grew swiftly into rhythm with the beats of the hymn. When, however, their goal rose, like a blazing star, over the undulation of the road, the volume of the chanting suddenly died away, leaving only the voices of the ringleaders, shouting indeed now somewhat out of tune, but, if anything, more vigorously than before. Their persistence and example nevertheless failed to prevent a perceptible breaking and slackening of the pace, as the Manse was neared, and when the gate was reached, the whole crowd came to a dead halt. Vague fear for the future had begotten the courage that had brought the villagers thus far: fear for the present now smothered its kindred birth. The intense blaze from the gaps in the death-like silent pile lit up rows of livid, hesitating faces: and a smothered, frightened sobbing broke out among the children. 'Well,' said Arthur Price Williams, addressing Jack Peters, with an expert assumption of the modest discipleship, 'what do we do *now*, Jack?' But Peters was regarding the Manse with manifest dubiety, and ignored the question. The Llyddwdd witch-find seemed to be suddenly aborting.

At this juncture old Pritchard suddenly pushed his way forward, gesticulating weirdly with his bony hands and long arms. '*What!*' he shouted, in broken notes, 'fear ye to smite when the Lord hateth? *Burn* the warlock!' And seizing a flambeau from Peters, he flung open the rickety gate and strode on down the drive, his torch leaving a coiling trail of scintillant sparks on the night wind. 'Burn the warlock,' screamed a shrill voice from the wavering crowd, and in a moment the gregarious human instinct had prevailed. With an outburst of incoherent, threatening voice, the mob poured after the fanatic.

Woe betide the Philosopher now! They expected barricaded doors; but with a groan of a conscious insufficiency, the hinge-rusted portals swung at the push of Pritchard. Blinded by the light, he hesitated for a second on the threshold, while his followers came crowding up behind him.

Those who were there say that they saw Dr Nebogipfel, standing in the toneless electric glare, on a peculiar erection of brass and ebony and ivory; and that he seemed to be smiling at them, half pityingly and half scornfully, as it is said martyrs are wont to smile. Some assert, moreover, that by his side was sitting a tall man, clad in ravenswing, and some even aver that this second man—whom others deny— bore on his face the likeness of the Reverend Elijah Ulysses Cook, while others declare that he resembled the description of the murdered Williams. Be that as it may, it must now go unproven for ever, for suddenly a wonderous thing smote the crowd as it swarmed in through the entrance. Pritchard pitched headlong on the floor senseless. While shouts and shrieks of anger, changed in mid utterance to yells of agonising fear, or to the mute gasp of heart-stopping horror: and then a frantic rush was made for the doorway.

For the calm, smiling doctor, and his quiet, black-clad companion, and the polished platform which upbore them, had vanished before their eyes!

How an Esoteric Story Became Possible

A silvery-foliaged willow by the side of a mere. Out of the cress-spangled waters below, rise clumps of sedge-blades, and among them glows the purple fleur-de-lys, and sapphire vapour of forget-me-nots. Beyond is a sluggish stream of water reflecting the intense blue of the moist Fenland sky; and beyond that a low osier-fringed eyot. This limits all the visible universe, save some scattered pollards and spear-like poplars showing against the violet distance. At the foot of the willow reclines the Author watching a copper butterfly fluttering from iris to iris.

Who can fix the colours of the sunset? Who can take a cast of flame? Let him essay to register the mutations of mortal thought as it wanders from a copper butterfly to the disembodied soul, and thence passes to spiritual motions and the vanishing of Dr Moses Nebogipfel and the Rev. Elijah Ulysses Cook from the world of sense.

As the author lay basking there and speculating, as another once did under the Budh tree, on mystic transmutations, a presence became apparent. There was a somewhat on the eyot between him and the purple horizon—an opaque reflecting entity, making itself dimly perceptible by reflection in the water to his averted eyes. He raised them in curious surprise.

What was it?

He stared in stupefied astonishment at the apparition, doubted, blinked, rubbed his eyes, stared again, and believed. It was solid, it cast a shadow, and it upbore two men. There was white metal in it that blazed in the noontide sun like incandescent magnesium, ebony bars that drank in the light, and white parts that gleamed like polished ivory. Yet withal it seemed unreal. The thing was not square as a machine ought to be, but all awry: it was twisted and seemed falling over, hanging in two directions, as those queer crystals called triclinic hang; it seemed like a machine that had been crushed or warped; it was suggestive and not confirmatory, like the machine of a disordered dream. The men, too, were dreamlike. One was short, intensely sallow, with a strangely-shaped head, and clad in a garment of dark olive green, the other was, grotesquely out of place, evidently a clergyman of the Established Church, a fair-haired, pale-faced respectable-looking man.

Once more doubt came rushing in on the author. He sprawled back and stared at the sky, rubbed his eyes, stared at the willow wands that hung between him and the blue, closely examined his hands to see if his eyes had any new things to relate about them, and then sat up again and stared at the eyot. A gentle breeze stirred the osiers; a white bird was flapping its way through the lower sky. The machine of the vision had vanished! It was an illusion—a projection of the subjective—an assertion of the immateriality of mind. 'Yes,' interpolated the sceptic faculty, 'but *how comes it that the clergyman is still there?*'

The clergyman had not vanished. In intense perplexity the author examined this black-coated phenomenon as he stood regarding the world with hand-shaded eyes. The author knew the periphery of that eyot by heart, and the question that troubled him was, 'Whence?' The clergyman looked as Frenchmen look when they land at Newhaven—intensely travel-worn; his clothes showed rubbed and seamy in the bright day. When he came to the edge of the island and shouted a question to the author, his voice was broken and trembled. 'Yes,' answered the author, 'it is an island. *How did you get there?*'

But the clergyman, instead of replying to this asked a very

strange question.

He said 'Are you in the nineteenth century?' The author made him repeat that question before he replied. 'Thank heaven,' cried the clergyman rapturously. Then he asked very eagerly for the exact date.

'August the ninth, eighteen hundred and eighty-seven,' he repeated after the author. 'Heaven be praised!' and sinking down on the eyot so that the sedges hid him, he audibly burst into tears.

Now the author was mightily surprised at all this, and going a certain distance along the mere, he obtained a punt, and getting into it he hastily poled to the eyot where he had last seen the clergyman. He found him lying insensible among the reeds, and carried him in his punt to the house where he lived, and the clergyman lay there insensible for ten days.

Meanwhile, it became known that he was the Rev. Elijah Cook, who had disappeared from Llyddwdd with Dr Moses Nebogipfel three weeks before.

On August 19th, the nurse called the author out of his study to speak to the invalid. He found him perfectly sensible, but his eyes were strangely bright, and his face was deadly pale. 'Have you found out who I am?' he asked.

'You are the Rev. Elijah Ulysses Cook, Master of Arts, of Pembroke College, Oxford, and Rector of Llyddwdd, near

Rwstog, in Caernarvon.'

He bowed his head. 'Have you been told anything of how I came here?'

'I found you among the reeds,' I said. He was silent and thoughtful for a while. 'I have a deposition to make. Will you take it? It concerns the murder of an old man named Williams, which occurred in 1862, this disappearance of Dr Moses Nebogipfel, the abduction of a ward in the year 4003—'

The author stared.

'The year of our Lord 4003,' he corrected. 'She would come. Also several assaults on public officials in the years 17,901 and 2.'

The author coughed.

'The years 17,901 and 2, and valuable medical, social, and physiographical data for all time.'

After a consultation with the doctor, it was decided to have the deposition taken down, and this is which constitutes the remainder of the story of the Chronic Argonauts.

On August 29th, 1887, the Rev Elijah Cook died. His body was conveyed to Llyddwdd, and buried in the churchyard there.

The Anachronic Man

Incidentally it has been remarked in the first part, how the Reverend Elijah Ulysses Cook attempted and failed to quiet the superstitious, excitement of the villagers on the afternoon of the memorable twenty-second of July. His next proceeding was to try and warn the unsocial philosopher of the dangers which impended. With this intent he made his way from the rumour-pelted village, through the silent, slumbrous heat of the July afternoon, up the slopes of Pen-y-pwll, to the old Manse. His loud knocking at the heavy door called forth dull resonance from the interior, and produced a shower of lumps of plaster and fragments of decaying touchwood from the rickety porch, but beyond this the dreamy stillness of the summer mid-day remained unbroken. Everything was so quiet as he stood there expectant, that the occasional speech of the haymakers a mile away in the fields, over towards Rwstog, could be distinctly heard. The reverend gentleman waited, then knocked again, and waited again, and listened, until the echoes and the patter of rubbish had melted away into the deep silence, and the creeping in the blood-vessels of his ears had become oppressively audible, swelling and sinking with sounds like the confused murmuring of a distant crowd, and causing a suggestion of anxious discomfort to spread slowly over his mind.

Again he knocked, this time loud, quick blows with his stick, and almost immediately afterwards, leaning his hand against the door, he kicked the panels vigorously. There was a shouting of echoes, a protesting jarring of hinges, and then the oaken door yawned and displayed, in the blue blaze of the electric light, vestiges of partitions, piles of planking and straw, masses of metal, heaps of papers and overthrown apparatus, to the rector's astonished eyes. 'Doctor Nebogipfel, excuse my intruding,' he called out, but the only response was a reverberation among the black beams and shadows that hung dimly above. For almost a minute he stood there, leaning forward over the threshold, staring at the glittering mechanisms, diagrams, books, scattered indiscriminately with broken food, packing cases, heaps of coke, hay, and microcosmic lumber, about the undivided house cavity; and then, removing his hat and treading stealthily, as if the silence were a sacred thing, he stepped into the apparently deserted shelter of the Doctor.

His eyes sought everywhere, as he cautiously made his way through the confusion, with a strange anticipation of finding Nebogipfel hidden somewhere in the sharp black shadows among the litter, so strong in him was an indescribable sense of perceiving presence. This feeling was so vivid that, when, after an abortive exploration, he seated himself upon Nebogipfel's diagram-covered bench, it made him explain in a forced hoarse voice to the stillness—'He is not here. I have something to say to him. I must wait for him.' It was so vivid, too, that the trickling of some grit down the wall in the vacant corner behind him made him start round in a sudden perspiration. There was nothing visible there, but turning his head back, he was stricken rigid with horror by the swift, noiseless apparition of Nebogipfel, ghastly pale, and with red stained hands, crouching upon a strange-looking metallic platform, and with his deep grey eyes looking intently into the visitor's face.

Cook's first impulse was to yell out his fear, but his throat was paralysed, and he could only stare fascinated at the bizarre countenance that had thus clashed suddenly into visibility. The lips were quivering and the breath came in short convulsive sobs. The un-human forehead was wet with perspiration, while the veins were swollen, knotted and purple. The Doctor's red hands, too, he noticed, were trembling, as the hands of slight people tremble after intense muscular exertion, and his lips closed and opened as if he, too, had a difficulty in speaking as he gasped, 'Who—what do you do here?'

Cook answered not a word, but stared with hair erect, open mouth, and dilated eyes, at the dark red unmistakeable smear that streaked the pure ivory and gleaming nickel and shining ebony of the platform.

'What are you doing here?' repeated the doctor, raising himself. 'What do you want?'

Cook gave a convulsive effort. 'In Heaven's name, *what are you?*' he gasped; and then black curtains came closing in from every side, sweeping the squatting, dwarfish phantasm that reeled before him into rayless, voiceless night.

The Reverend Elijah Ulysses Cook recovered his perceptions to find himself lying on the floor of the old Manse, and Doctor Nebogipfel, no longer blood-stained and with all trace of his agitation gone, kneeling by his side and bending over him with a glass of brandy in his hand. 'Do not be alarmed, sir,' said the philosopher with a faint smile, as the clergyman opened his eyes. 'I have not treated you to a disembodied spirit, or anything nearly so extraordinary . . . may I offer you this?'

The clergyman submitted quietly to the brandy, and then stared perplexed into Nebogipfel's face, vainly searching his memory for what occurrences had preceded his insensibility. Raising himself at last, into a sitting posture, he saw the oblique mass of metals that had appeared with the doctor, and immediately all that happened flashed back upon his mind. He looked from this structure to the recluse, and from the recluse to the structure.

'There is absolutely no deception, sir,' said Nebogipfel with the slightest trace of mockery in his voice. 'I lay no claim to work in matters spiritual. It is a *bona fide* mechanical contrivance, a thing emphatically of this sordid world. Excuse me—just one minute.' He rose from his knees, stepped upon the mahogany platform, took a curiously curved lever in his hand and pulled it over. Cook rubbed his eyes. *There* certainly was no deception. The doctor and the machine had vanished.

The reverend gentleman felt no horror this time, only a slight nervous shock, to see the doctor presently re-appear 'in the twinkling of an eye' and get down from the machine. From that he walked in a straight line with his hands behind his back and his face downcast, until his progress was stopped by the intervention of a circular saw; then, turning round sharply on his heel, he said:

'I was thinking while I was . . . away . . . Would you like to come? I should greatly value a companion.'

The clergyman was still sitting, hatless, on the floor. 'I am afraid,' he said slowly, 'you will think me stupid—'

'Not at all,' interrupted the doctor. 'The stupidity is mine. You desire to have all this explained . . . wish to know where I am going first. I have spoken so little with men of this age for the last ten years or more that I have ceased to make due allowances and concessions for other minds. I will do my best, but that I fear will be very unsatisfactory. It is a long story . . . do you find that floor comfortable to sit on? If not, there is a nice packing case over there, or some straw behind you, or this bench—the diagrams are done with now, but I am afraid of the drawing pins. You may sit on the Chronic Argo!'

'No, thank you,' slowly replied the clergyman, eyeing that deformed structure thus indicated, suspiciously; 'I am *quite* comfortable here.'

'Then I will begin. Do you read fables? Modern ones?'

'I am afraid I must confess to a good deal of fiction,' said the clergyman deprecatingly. 'In Wales the ordained ministers of the sacraments of the Church have perhaps *too* large a share of leisure—'

'Have you read the Ugly Duckling?'

'Hans Christian Andersen's—yes—in my childhood.'

'A wonderful story—a story that has ever been full of tears and heart swelling hopes for me, since first it came to me in my lonely boyhood and saved me from unspeakable things. That story, if you understand it well, will tell you almost all that you should know of me to comprehend how that machine came to be thought of in a mortal brain . . . Even when I read that simple narrative for the first time, a thousand bitter experiences had begun the teaching of my isolation among the people of my birth—I knew the story was for me. The ugly duckling that proved to be a swan, that lived through all contempt and bitterness, to float at last sublime. From that hour forth, I dreamt of meeting with my kind, dreamt of encountering that sympathy I knew was my profoundest need. Twenty years I lived in that hope, lived and worked, lived and wandered, loved even, and at last, despaired. Only once among all those millions of wondering, astonished, indifferent, contemptuous, and insidious faces that I met with in that passionate wandering, looked *one* upon me as I desired . . . looked—'

He paused. The Reverend Cook glanced up into his face, expecting some indication of the deep feeling that had sounded in his last words. It was downcast, clouded, and thoughtful, but the mouth was rigidly firm.

'In short, Mr Cook, I discovered that I was one of those superior Cagots called a genius—a man born out of my time—a man thinking the thoughts of a wiser age, doing things and believing things that men now *cannot* understand, and that in the years ordained to me there was nothing but silence and suffering for my soul—unbroken solitude, man's bitterest pain. I knew I was an Anachronic Man; my age was still to come. One filmy hope alone held me to life, a hope to which I clung until it had become a certain thing. Thirty years of unremitting toil and deepest thought among the hidden things of matter and form and life, and then *that*, the Chronic Argo, *the ship that sails through time*, and now I go to join my generation, to journey through the ages till my time has come.'

The Chronic Argo

Dr Nebogipfel paused, looked in sudden doubt at the clergyman's perplexed face. 'You think that sounds mad,' he said, 'to travel through time?'

'It certainly jars with accepted opinions,' said the clergyman, allowing the faintest suggestion of controversy to appear in his intonation, and speaking apparently to the Chronic Argo. Even a clergyman of the Church of England you see can have a suspicion of illusions at times.

'It certainly *does* jar with accepted opinions,' agreed the philosopher cordially. 'It does more than that—it defies accepted opinions to mortal combat. Opinions of all sorts, Mr Cook—Scientific Theories, Laws, Articles of Belief, or, to come to elements, Logical Premises, Ideas, or whatever you like to call them—all are, from the infinite nature of things, so many diagrammatic caricatures of the ineffable—caricatures altogether to be avoided save where they are necessary in the shaping of results—as chalk outlines are necessary to the painter and plans and sections to the engineer. Men, from the exigencies of their being, find this hard to believe.'

The Rev. Elijah Ulysses Cook nodded his head with the quiet smile of one whose opponent has unwittingly given a point.

'It is as easy to come to regard ideas as complete reproductions of entities as it is to roll off a log. Hence it is that almost all civilised men believe in the *reality* of the Greek geometrical conceptions.'

'Oh! pardon me, sir,' interrupted Cook. 'Most men know that a geometrical point has no existence in matter, and the same with a geometrical line. I think you underrate . . .'

'Yes, yes, *those* things are recognised,' said Nebogipfel calmly; 'but now . . . a cube. Does that exist in the material universe?'

'Certainly.'

'An instantaneous cube?'

'I don't know what you intend by that expression.'

'Without any other sort of extension; a body having length, breadth, and thickness, exists?'

'What other sort of extension *can* there be?' asked Cook, with raised eyebrows.

'Has it never occurred to you that no form can exist in the material universe that has no extension in time? . . . Has it never glimmered upon your consciousness that nothing stood between men and a geometry of four dimensions—

length, breadth, thickness, and *duration*—but the inertia of opinion, the impulse from the Levantine philosophers of the bronze age?'

'Putting it that way,' said the clergyman, 'it does look as though there was a flaw somewhere in the notion of tridimensional being; but' . . . He became silent, leaving that sufficiently eloquent 'but' to convey all the prejudice and distrust that filled his mind.

'When we take up this new light of a fourth dimension and reexamine our physical science in its illumination,' continued Nebogipfel, after a pause, 'we find ourselves no longer limited by hopeless restriction to a certain beat of time—to our own generation. Locomotion along lines of duration—chronic navigation comes within the range, first, of geometrical theory, and then of practical mechanics. There *was* a time when men could only move horizontally and in their appointed country. The clouds floated above them, unattainable things, mysterious chariots of those fearful gods who dwelt among the mountain summits. Speaking practically, men in those days were restricted to motion in two dimensions; and even there circumambient ocean and hypoborean fear bound him in. But those times were to pass away. First, the keel of Jason cut its way between the Symplegades, and then in the fulness of time, Columbus dropped anchor in a bay of Atlantis. Then man burst his bidimensional limits, and invaded the third dimension, soaring with Montgolfier into the clouds, and sinking with a diving bell into the purple treasure-caves of the waters. And now another step, and the hidden past and unknown future are before us. We stand upon a mountain summit with the plains of the ages spread below.'

Nebogipfel paused and looked down at his hearer.

The Reverend Elijah Cook was sitting with an expression of strong distrust on his face. Preaching much had brought home certain truths to him very vividly, and he always suspected rhetoric. 'Are those things figures of speech,' he asked; 'or am I to take them as precise statements? Do you speak of travelling through time in the same way as one might speak of Omnipotence making His pathway on the storm, or do you—a—mean what you say?'

Dr Nebogipfel smiled quietly. 'Come and look at these diagrams,' he said, and then with elaborate simplicity he commenced to explain again to the clergyman the new quadridimensional geometry. Insensibly Cook's aversion passed away, and seeming impossibility grew possible, now that such tangible things as diagrams and models could be brought forward in evidence. Presently he found himself asking questions, and his interest grew deeper and deeper as Nebogipfel slowly and with precise clearness unfolded the beautiful order of his strange invention. The moments slipped away unchecked, as the Doctor passed on to the narrative of his research, and it was with a start of surprise that the clergyman noticed the deep blue of the dying twilight through the open doorway.

'The voyage,' said Nebogipfel concluding his history, 'will be full of undreamt-of dangers—already in one brief essay I have stood in the very jaws of death—but it is also full of the divinest promise of undreamt-of joy. Will you come? Will you walk among the people of the Golden Years? . . .'

But the mention of death by the philosopher had brought flooding back to the mind of Cook, all the horrible sensations of that first apparition.

'Dr Nebogipfel . . . one question?' He hesitated. 'On your hands . . . *Was it blood?*'

Nebogipfel's countenance fell. He spoke slowly.

'When I had stopped my machine, I found myself in this room as it used to be. *Hark!*'

'It is the wind in the trees towards Rwstog.'

'It sounded like the voices of a multitude of people singing . . . when I had stopped I found myself in this room as it used to be. An old man, a young man, and a lad were sitting at a table—reading some book together. I stood behind them unsuspected. "Evil spirits assailed him," read the old man; "but it is written, 'to him that overcometh shall be given life eternal'. They came as entreating friends, but he

84

endured through all their snares. They came as principalities and powers, but he defied them in the name of the King of Kings. Once even it is told that in his study, while he was translating the New Testament into German, the Evil One himself appeared before him . . ." Just then the lad glanced timorously round, and with a fearful wail fainted away . . .

'The others sprang at me . . . It was a fearful grapple . . . The old man clung to my throat, screaming "Man or Devil, I defy thee . . ."

'I could not help it. We rolled together on the floor . . . the knife his trembling son had dropped came to my hand . . . Hark!'

He paused and listened, but Cook remained staring at him in the same horror-stricken attitude he had assumed when the memory of the blood-stained hands had rushed back over his mind.

'Do you hear what they are crying? *Hark!*

Burn the warlock! Burn the murderer!

'Do you hear? There is no time to be lost.'

Slay the murderer of cripples. Kill the devil's claw!

'Come! Come!'

Cook, with a convulsive effort, made a gesture of repugnance and strode to the doorway. A crowd of black figures roaring towards him in the red torchlight made him recoil. He shut the door and faced Nebogipfel.

The thin lips of the Doctor curled with a contemptuous sneer. 'They will kill you if you stay,' he said; and seizing his unresisting vistior by the wrist, he forced him towards the glittering machine. Cook sat down and covered his face with his hands.

In another moment the door was flung open, and old Pritchard stood blinking on the threshold.

A pause. A hoarse shout changing suddenly into a sharp shrill shriek.

A thunderous roar like the bursting forth of a great fountain of water.

The voyage of the Chronic Argonauts had begun.

MERLIN AND THE MAGICIANS

Geoffrey of Monmouth

It then came about that King Vortigern, not knowing what to do against the barbarians who were causing such desolation throughout his land, retired into Cambria to consider his future and what he should do.

At last he had recourse to magicians for their advice, and commanded them to tell him what course to take. They advised him to build a very strong tower for his own safety, since he had lost all his other fortified places. Accordingly he made a progress about the country, to find out a convenient situation, and came at last to Mount Erir [Snowdon], where he assembled workmen from several countries, and ordered them to build the tower.

The builders, therefore, began to lay the foundation; but whatever they did one day, the earth swallowed up the next, so as to leave no appearance of their work. Vortigern, being informed of this, again consulted with his magicians concerning the cause of it, who told him that he must find out a youth that never had a father, and kill him, and then sprinkle the stones and cement with his blood; for by those means, they said, he would have a firm foundation.

Hereupon messengers were forthwith dispatched away over all the provinces, to inquire out such a man. In their travels they came to a city, called afterwards Kaermerdin [Carmarthen], where they saw some young men, playing before the gate, and went up to them. But being weary with their journey, they sat down in the ring, to see if they could meet with what they were in quest of.

Towards evening, there happened on a sudden a quarrel between two of the young men, whose names were Merlin and Dabutius. In the dispute, Dabutius said to Merlin: 'You fool, do you presume to quarrel with me? Is there any equality in our birth? I am descended of royal race, both by my father and mother's side. As for you, nobody knows what you are, for you never had a father.'

At that word the messengers looked earnestly on Merlin, and asked the by-standers who he was. They told him, it was not known who was his father; but that his mother was daughter to the king of Demetia, and that she lived in St Peter's Church among the nuns of that city.

Upon this the messengers hastened to the governor of the city, and ordered him, in the king's name, to send Merlin and his mother to the king. As soon as the governor understood the occasion of their message, he readily obeyed the order and sent them to Vortigern to complete his design.

When they were introduced into the king's presence, he received the mother in a very respectful manner, on account of her noble birth; and began to inquire of her by what man she had conceived.

'My sovereign lord,' said she, 'by the life of your soul and mine, I know nobody that begot him of me. Only this I know, that as I was once with my companions in our chambers, there appeared to me a person in the shape of a most beautiful young man, who often embraced me eagerly in his arms, and kissed me; and when he had stayed a little time, he suddenly vanished out of my sight. But many times after this he would talk with me when I sat alone, without making any visible appearance.

'When he had a long time haurted me in this manner, he at last lay with me several times in the shape of a man, and left me with child. And I do affirm to you, my sovereign lord, that excepting that young man, I know no body begot him of me.'

The king, full of admiration at this account, ordered Maugantius to be called, that he might satisfy him as to the possibility of what the woman had related. Maugantius being introduced, and having the whole matter repeated to him, said to Vortigern:

'In the books of our philosophers, and in a great many

histories, I have found that several men have had the like original. For, as Apuleius informs us in his book concerning the Demon of Socrates, between the moon and the earth inhabit those spirits, which we call incubuses. These are of the nature partly of men, and partly of angels, and whenever they please assume human shapes, and lie with women. Perhaps one of them appeared to this woman, and begot that young man of her.'

Merlin, in the mean time was attentive to all that had passed, and then approached the king, and said to him, 'For what reason am I and my mother introduced into your presence?'

'My magicians,' answered Vortigern, 'advised me to seek out a man that had no father, with whose blood my building is to be sprinkled, in order to make it stand.'

'Order your magicians,' said Merlin, 'to come before me, and I will convict them of a lie.'

The king was surprised at his words, and presently ordered the magicians to come, and sit down before Merlin, who spoke to them after this manner: 'Because you are ignorant what it is that hinders the foundation of the tower, you have recommended the shedding of my blood for cement to it, as if that would presently make it stand. But tell me now, what is there under the foundation? For something there is that will not suffer it to stand.'

The magicians at this began to be afraid, and made him no answer. Then said Merlin. 'I entreat your majesty would command your workmen to dig into the ground, and you will find a pond deep under ground which had made it give way.'

Merlin after this went again to the magicians, and said, 'Tell me, ye false sycophants, what is there under the pond?' But they were silent.

Then said he again to the king, 'Command the pond to be drained, and at the bottom you will see two hollow stones, and in them two dragons asleep.'

The king made no scruple of believing him, since he had found true what he said of the pond and therefore ordered it to be drained: which done, he found as Merlin had said; and now was possessed with the greatest admiration of him. Nor were the rest that were present less amazed at his wisdom, thinking it to be no less than divine inspiration.

And thereafter his wisdom was much sought by all of high and low estate; and many and amazing were his predictions.

LLUDD AND LLEVELYS

Anonymous

(Traditional)

Beli the Great, the son of Manogan, had three sons, Lludd
and Caswallawn and Nynyaw, and according to the story
he had a fourth son called Llevelys. And after the death of
Beli, the kingdom of the Island of Britain fell into the hands
of Lludd, his eldest son; and Lludd ruled prosperously, and
rebuilt the walls of London, and encompassed it about with
numberless towers. And after that he bade the citizens build
houses therein, such as no houses in the kingdom could
equal. And moreover he was a mighty warrior, and generous
and liberal in giving meat and drink to all that sought them.
And though he had many castles and cities, this one loved
he more than any. And he dwelt therein most part of the
year, and therefore was it called Caer Lludd, and at last Caer
London. And after the stranger-race came there, it was called
London, or Lwndrys.

Lludd loved Llevelys best of all his brothers, because he
was a wise and discreet man. Having heard that the King

92

of France had died, leaving no heir except a daughter, and that he had left all his possessions in her hands, he came to Lludd his brother to beseech his counsel and aid; and that not so much for his own welfare as to seek to add to the glory and honour and dignity of his kindred, if he might go to France to woo the maiden for his wife. And forthwith his brother conferred with him, and this counsel was pleasing unto him.

So he prepared ships, and filled them with armed knights, and set forth towards France. And as soon as they had landed, they sent messengers to show the nobles of France the cause of the embassy. And by the joint counsel of the nobles of France and of the princes, the maiden was given to Llevelys, and the crown of the kingdom with her. And thenceforth he ruled the land discreetly and wisely and happily as long as his life lasted.

After a space of time had passed, three plagues fell on the Island of Britain, such as none in the islands had ever seen the like of. The first was a certain race that came, and was called the Coranians; and so great was their knowledge, that there was no discourse upon the face of the island, however low it might be spoken, but what, if the wind met it, it was known to them. And through this they could not be injured.

The second plague was a shriek which came on every Mayeve over every hearth in the Island of Britain. And this went through people's hearts, and so scared them, that the men lost their hue and their strength, and the young men and the maidens lost their senses, and all the animals and trees, and the earth and the waters, were left barren.

The third plague was, that, however much of provisions and food might be prepared in the king's courts, were there even so much as a year's provision of meat and drink, none of it could ever be found, except what was consumed in the first night. And two of these plagues no one ever knew their cause, therefore was there better hope of being freed from the first than from the second and third.

And thereupon King Lludd felt greater sorrow and care, because that he knew not how he might be freed from these plagues. And he called to him all the nobles of his kingdom, and asked counsel of them what they should do against these afflictions. And by the common counsel of the nobles, Lludd the son of Beli went to Llevelys his brother, King of France, for he was a man great of counsel and wisdom, to seek his advice.

And they made ready a fleet, and that in secret and in silence, lest that race should know the cause of their errand, or any besides the king and his counsellors. And when they were made ready, they went into their ships, Lludd and those he chose with him. And they began to cleave the seas towards France.

And when these tidings came to Llevelys, seeing that he knew not the cause of his brother's ships he came on the other side to meet him, and with him was a fleet vast of size. And when Lludd saw this, he left all the ships out upon the sea except one only; and in that one he came to meet his brother, and he likewise with a single ship came to meet him. And when they were come together, each put his arms about the other's neck, and they welcomed each other with brotherly love.

After that Lludd had shown his brother the cause of his errand, Llevelys said that he himself knew the cause of the coming to those lands. And they took counsel together to discourse on the matter otherwise than thus, in order that the wind might not catch their words, nor the Coranians know what they might say. Then Llevelys caused a long horn to be made of brass, and through this horn they discoursed. But whatsoever words they spoke through this horn, one to the other, neither of them could hear any other but harsh and hostile words. And when Llevelys saw this, and that there was a demon thwarting them, and disturbing through this horn, he caused wine to be put therein to wash it. And through the virtue of the wine the demon was driven out of the horn. And when their discourse was unobstructed, Llevelys told his brother that he would give him some insects, whereof he should keep some to breed, lest by chance the like affliction might come a second time. And other of these insects he should take and bruise in water. And he assured him that it would have power to destroy the race of the Coranians. That is to say, that when he came home to his kingdom, he should call together all the people, both of his own race and of the race of the Coranians, for a conference, as though with the intent of making peace between them, and that when they were all together he should take his charmed water, and cast it over all alike. And he assured him that the water would poison the race of the Coranians, but that it would not slay or harm those of his own race.

'And the second plague,' said he, 'that is in thy dominion, behold it is a dragon. And another dragon of a foreign race is fighting with it, and striving to overcome it. And therefore does your dragon make a fearful outcry. And on this wise mayest thou come to know this. After thou hast returned home, cause the island to be measured in its length and breadth; and in the place where thou dost find the exact central point, there cause a pit to be dug, and cause a cauldron full of the best mead that can be made to be put in the pit, with a covering of satin over the face of the cauldron. And then in thine own person do thou remain there watching, and thou wilt see the dragons fighting in the form of terrific animals. And at length they will take the form of dragons in the air. And last of all, after wearying themselves with fierce and furious fighting, they will fall, in the form of two pigs, upon the covering, and they will sink in, and the covering with them, and they will draw it down to the very bottom of the cauldron. And they will drink up the whole of the mead; and after that they will sleep. Thereupon do thou immediately fold the covering around them, and bury them in a *kistvaen* in the strongest place thou hast in thy dominions, and hide them in the earth. And as long as they shall bide in that strong place, no plague shall come to the Island of Britain from elsewhere.

'The cause of the third plague,' said he, 'is a mighty man of magic, who takes thy meat and thy drink and thy store. And he, through illusions and charms, causes every one to sleep. Therefore it is needful for thee in thy own person to watch thy food and thy provisions. And lest he should overcome thee with sleep, be there a cauldron of cold water by thy side, and when thou art oppressed with sleep, plunge into the cauldron.'

Then Lludd returned back unto his land. And immediately he summoned to him the whole of his own race and of the Coranians. And, as Llevelys had taught him, he bruised the insects in water, the which he cast over them all together, and forthwith it destroyed the whole tribe of the Coranians, without hurt to any of the Britons.

And some time after this Lludd caused the island to be measured in its length and in its breadth. And in Oxford he found the central point, and in that place he caused the earth to be dug, and in that pit a cauldron to be set full of the best mead that could be made, and a covering of-satin over the face of it. And he himself watched that night. And while he was there, he beheld the dragons fighting. And when they were weary they fell, and came down upon the top of the satin, and drew it with them to the bottom of the cauldron. And when they had drunk the mead they slept. And in their sleep Lludd folded the covering around them, and in the securest place he had in Snowdon he hid them in a *kistvaen*. Now after that, this spot was called Dinas Emrys, but before that, Dinas Ffaraon. And thus the fierce outcry ceased in his dominions.

And when this was ended, King Lludd caused an exceeding great banquet to be prepared. And when it was ready, he placed a vessel of cold water by his side, and he in his own proper person watched it. And as he abode thus clad with arms, about the third watch of the night, lo, he heard many surpassing fascinations and various songs. And drowsiness urged him to sleep. Upon this, lest he should be hindered from his purpose, and be overcome by sleep, he went often into the water. And at last, behold a man of vast size, clad in strong, heavy armour came in, bearing a hamper. And as he was wont, he put all the food and provisions of meat and drink into the hamper, and proceeded to go with it forth. And nothing was ever more wonderful to Lludd than that the hamper should hold so much.

And thereupon King Lludd went after him, and spoke unto him thus: 'Stop, stop,' said he, 'though thou hast done many insults and much spoil erewhile, thou shalt not do so any more, unless thy skill in arms and thy prowess be greater than mine.'

Then he instantly put down the hamper on the floor, and awaited him. And a fierce encounter was between them, so that the glittering fire flew out from their arms. And at the last Lludd grappled with him, and fate bestowed the victory on Lludd. And he threw the plague to the earth. And after he had overcome him by strength and might he besought his mercy.

'How can I grant thee mercy,' said the king, 'after all the many injuries and wrongs that thou hast done me?'

'All the losses that ever I have caused thee,' said he, 'I will make thee atonement for, equal to what I have taken. And I will never do the like from this time forth. But thy faithful vassal will I be.'

And the king accepted this from him.

Giraldus Cambrensis

Giraldus Cambrensis was born in Manorbier, Wales, sometime between 1145 and 1147. He received his early education from his uncle, the bishop of St. Davids, before studying at the University of Paris. Upon his return in 1172, he received a commission from Richard, the archbishop of Canterbury, to enforce the payment of tithes on wool and cheese in the diocese of St. Davids. Some years later, Cambrensis returned to Paris, and from 1184 found himself associated with the king and court of England, whom he accompanied on many trips to Ireland. His most famous works are two descriptive works on Ireland – *Topographia Hibernica* (1187) and *Expugnatio Hibernica* (1189) – and one on Wales, entitled *Descriptio Cambriae* (1194). These texts include valuable glimpses of medieval life and folklore. Cambrensis also completed biographies of a number of saints, bishops and other religious figures; indeed, he spent his whole life battling and failing to become Archbishop of St. David's himself. Cambrensis died circa 1223.

Arthur Machen

Arthur Machen was born in Caerleon, Monmouthshire, Wales in 1863. At the age of eleven, he boarded at Hereford Cathedral School, where he received a comprehensive classical education. Family poverty ruled out going to university, and Machen was sent to London, where he sat entrance exams at medical school but failed to get in. In the capital, he lived in relative poverty, working in a variety of short-lived jobs and exploring the city during the evenings. However, he began to show literary promise; in 1881, at the age of just eighteen, he published a long poem, 'Eleusinia', and in 1884, he published his second work, the pastiche *The Anatomy of Tobacco*.

By 1890, Machen was publishing in literary magazines, and writing stories with Gothic and fantastic themes. His first major success came in 1894, with the novella *The Great God Pan*. Although widely denounced by the press as degenerate and horrific because of its decadent style and sexual content, it has since garnered a reputation as a classic of horror; indeed, author Stephen King has called it "maybe the best [horror story] in the English language." Machen next produced *The Three Impostors* (1895), a novel composed of a number of interwoven tales which are now regarded as some of his best works.

Between 1900 and 1910, Machen dabbled in acting, and published what is generally seen as his *magnum opus, The Hill of Dreams* (1907). He accepted a full-time journalist's job at Alfred Harmsworth's *Evening News* in 1910, where he remained throughout the war, not leaving until 1921. Machen accepted this role mainly to pay his bills – fiction-writing was his true passion, and he carried on producing novels and short stories throughout the 1910s – but he came to be regarded as a great Fleet Street character by his contemporaries.

The early 1920s saw something of a Machen boom; his works became popular in America, and he brought out his two-volume autobiography. However, by 1929 he was struggling financially again, and left London with his family. It was only a literary appeal launched on the occasion of his eightieth birthday – which drew contributions from admirers such as T. S. Eliot and Bernard Shaw – that eventually ended Machen's money woes. He died some years later in Beaconsfield, Buckinghamshire, England, aged 84. His legacy remains formidable; his work has influenced countless other artists, and is seen as setting the stage for – amongst other things – the Cthulhu horrors of H. P. Lovecraft.

Geoffrey of Monmouth

Geoffrey of Monmouth was born circa 1100. Little is known about the details of his life, but it is widely believed that he was an Oxford cleric for most of his life, possibly at St. George's church. His largely fictionalised *History of the Kings of Britain* (c. 1135-39) traced the descent of British nobility from the Trojans; it brought the figures of Arthur and the enchanter Merlin into European literature. Though denounced from the first by other historians, the work was one of the most popular books of the Middle Ages and had a great influence on later chroniclers. Geoffrey died in 1155.

H. G. Wells

Herbert George Wells was born in Bromley, England in 1866. He apprenticed as a draper before becoming a pupil-teacher at Midhurst Grammar School in West Sussex. Some years later, Wells won a scholarship to the School of Science in London, where he developed a strong interest in biology and evolution, founding and editing the *Science Schools Journal*. However, he left before graduating to return to teaching, and began to focus increasingly on writing. His first major essay on science, 'The Rediscovery of the Unique', appeared in 1891. However, it was in 1895 that Wells seriously established himself as a writer, with the publication of the now iconic novel, *The Time Machine*.

Wells followed *The Time Machine* with the equally well-received *War of the Worlds* (1898), which proved highly popular in the USA, and was serialized in the magazine *Cosmopolitan*. Around the turn of the century, he also began to write extensively on politics, technology and the future, producing works *The Discovery of the Future* (1902) and *Mankind in the Making* (1903). An active socialist, in 1904 Wells joined the Fabian Society, and his 1905 book *A Modern Utopia* presented a vision of a socialist society founded on reason and compassion. Wells also penned a range of successful comic novels, such as *Kipps* (1905) and *The History of Mr Polly* (1910).

Wells' 1920 work, *The Outline of History*, was penned in response to the Russian Revolution, and declared that world would be improved by education, rather than revolution. It made Wells one of the most important political thinkers of the twenties and thirties, and he began to write for a number of journals and newspapers, even travelling to Russia to lecture Lenin and Trotsky on social reform. Appalled by the carnage of World War II, Wells began to work on a project dealing with the perils of nuclear war, but died before completing it. He is now regarded as one of the greatest science-fiction writers of all time, and an important political thinker.

www.ingramcontent.com/pod-product-compliance
Lightning Source LLC
Chambersburg PA
CBHW060406030726
47497CB00003B/867